The Language of the Dragon

Dragon Speech Book 1

Margaret Ball

Galway Publishing

Published by Galway Publishing

ISBN Paperback: 978-1-947648-20-3
ISBN eBook: 978-1-947648-21-0

Printed in the United States of America
Cover art: Cedar Sanderson
Formatting: Polgarus Studio

Also by Margaret Ball:

The Applied Topology series

A Pocketful of Stars (Book 1)

An Opening in the Air (Book 2)

An Annoyance of Grackles (Book 3)

A Tapestry of Fire (Book 4)

A Creature of Smokeless Flame (Book 5)

A Revolution of Rubies (Book 6)

A Child of Magic (forthcoming 2019)

The Dragon Speech series

The Language of the Dragon

Dragon Scales (forthcoming 2019)

The Harmony series

Insurgents (Book 1)

Awakening (Book 2)

Survivors (Book 3)

Other books

Disappearing Act

Duchess of Aquitaine

Mathemagics

Lost in Translation

No Earthly Sunne

Changeweaver

Flameweaver

The Shadow Gate

The Language of the Dragon

1. Crazy lady with a cannon

After the long, hot drive back to Austin from Port Aransas, I decided to skip dinner in favor of a nice long shower and falling into bed. It was late anyway, and not bothering with dinner would save me the trouble of finding something in the pantry, cooking it, and washing up afterwards. Totally worth it. I still had sand between my toes.

While using up the house's hot water supply, I reflected peacefully on the benefits of my week-long escape. My mind was made up now: there was no way I was going to let Craig move in with me under the pretext of renting the vacant room on the other side of my bathroom. In fact, if I could swing it financially I just might not rent that room out at all. The previous tenant, Koshan, had turned out to be a nice enough guy right up until he took off without paying the last three weeks of his rent, but sharing a bathroom with a total stranger had made me feel *crowded*. Better to refurnish it as a nice little private sitting-room and claim that whole side of the house for myself, the way my friend and long-term tenant Laura had done with her side.

I dried off, slipped into a long cool nightgown of super-thin white lawn and wrapped a towel around my hair. Sat down on the bed to give some serious attention to my fingernails...

... And heard a clunking sound from the bathroom I'd just vacated.

Oh, well. It was probably Cath Palug, expressing his dissatisfaction at having been left with only Laura to take care of him for a week. He'd knock a certain number of things off flat surfaces before condescending to knead my chest and purr.

A louder clunk was followed by a string of curses.

I froze, and all the little hairs on my arms stood up. The week before leaving for the beach, I'd chased a daytime burglar out of the house. Had he come back to try his luck at night? It certainly wasn't possible to write the voice off as the doings of a disgruntled cat-monster. Nor was it my absconding tenant come back without warning. His voice had been higher, and his English not so smooth. Whoever was cursing was clearly fluent in English. Certain kinds of English, anyway.

I reached into my bag and retrieved my cell phone, held it up in front of my face and waited for my new app to unlock the phone.

No dice. It didn't recognize me with a towel wrapped around my wet hair. I *knew* I shouldn't have let Blossom talk me into installing that oh-so-convenient facial recognition app. She'd pointed out how it would save me the trouble of typing a passcode every time I used the phone. And I'm such a sucker for saving trouble, I actually took the advice of a girl called Blossom with a twin sister named Floss.

Setting the phone down, I reached down between the mattress and the box spring where I'd just stashed my other favored accessory. The one I started keeping handy after I decided that no one was ever going to invade my space again. I tiptoed to the bathroom door, threw it open and took a two-handed shooting stance. "Hands up and behind your head!" I shouted.

A white-faced stranger straightened up from the sink, banged his head on the open door of the medicine cabinet, raised his hands and slowly backed away from me.

Well, so much for the faint hope that it had only been Craig, seriously overstepping his bounds and earning a well-deserved shock. I'd never seen this man before.

He was young, well, about my age anyway. Average height, dark hair, blue eyes, jaw nearly blue with what looked like permanent five o'clock shadow. Might have been good-looking if he hadn't been white and shaking. Not that I minded. Terrified was, in my view, a very good look on men who sneaked into my house in the middle of the night.

"Who are you and what are you doing here?" I demanded.

"Lady, I don't know what you think you're—"

"I'm asking the questions here!" I interrupted with a little twitch of my Smith and Wesson .38 Special to emphasize the situation.

"Look, lady, I *paid* for my room, and if there's some kind of house rule about not using the bathroom that opens right out of my bedroom, somebody should have mentioned it, okay? And do you have to keep pointing that thing at my face?"

I lowered the gun until it was pointing at his legs. "You paid?"

"First and last month's rent *and* deposit. And who the fuck are you, anyway, crazy lady? Does the landlady know you run around threatening the other tenants with that baby cannon?"

"You know the landlady?"

"Nice lady. Georgia Brown. She—"

I lowered the gun even more, to point at the floor. My breathing was just beginning to get back to normal. "No, she was just the rental agent. *I'm* your landlady – Sienna Brown, her niece. This is my house."

"Yeah? I bet you get a rapid turnover in lodgers if you greet them all by shoving a gun in their faces. Crazy lady."

"You startled me. I've been out of town. I didn't know the room had been rented."

"Well, I'll be very careful not to startle you again," he said. Some color was beginning to come back into his face. "Can I put my hands down?"

"Oh, go ahead."

"My name is Michael Ryan," he said, cautiously lowering his hands an inch at a time, "and I can show you my copy of the rental agreement if you'll let me go back into my room and unpack it."

I went with him; I wasn't ready to let him out of my sight yet. I was startled anew by the sight of Koshan's clothes spilling out of an open carton. "Who told you that you could mess with the previous tenant's effects?"

"That wasn't me," he said promptly, "it was that way when I moved in this afternoon. I was going to talk to Georgia about getting that stuff out of my way, actually."

His eyes shifted around the room while he told me this. I had a feeling he was lying, but couldn't figure out why he'd bother. It's not like Koshan had owned anything worth stealing; even the people who had broken into that room, the week before I went to the beach, hadn't bothered to take any of his stuff.

I looked at the rental agreement. It was solid. Naturally. My aunt was a professional; she didn't do sloppy work. Renting out rooms in a house wasn't, strictly speaking, a realtor's job, but Aunt Georgia had rental property of her own and, being the efficient and competent type she was, managed it herself. She'd probably felt she was doing me a favor by managing my own property while I hid out at Port Aransas.

What it added up to was, I'd have some trouble evicting him. A lot of trouble, possibly, if he decided to hire a lawyer and make a big deal about the fact that I'd been a little bit startled to hear him in the bathroom. I handed it back to him.

"Okay, you can stay—for now. We can go over house rules in the morning."

"Like 'Don't surprise the landlady, she's crazy,'" he muttered. Not quite under his breath; just low enough that I would seem quarrelsome if I picked up on it.

Back in my own room, I shot the bolt that prevented anybody coming through from the shared bathroom. Then, after thinking it over, I fished a tissue out of my purse, crumpled it up and stuffed it into the keyhole whose key had been lost when I was in grade school. Then I replaced the gun and lay back on the bed. After that episode, it was going to be a long time before I got to sleep.

Cath Palug had been waiting on top of the tall bookcase. He launched now and landed hard on the bed, all four legs out and stiff. It was the kind of maneuver he executed to add bruises to his vocal complaints about life. Fortunately, he was kind of predictable; I'd started rolling over as soon as I glimpsed the yellowish-gray fluff at the top of the shelves. Immediately after hitting the mattress, he executed a sideways fall against the small of my back. I reached behind myself and shoved. You couldn't let Cath Palug start pushing you around; he'd once pushed me clean off the bed with a series of those sudden collapses, edging me a few inches at a time until my last move took me right off the mattress.

"Cut it out," I whispered. "Laura fed you already."

He kneaded my back, deploying claws.

Sighing, I rolled back towards him and skritched under his chin. How come everybody up to and including a previously homeless cat could push me around so easily?

Well, my life had been excessively complicated ever since I let an old client who'd become a friend talk me into a short-term rental to her foreign friend. First Koshan had been bouncing around some conference on campus and inviting total strangers to visit him here; then he'd disappeared and somebody had broken into the house to ransack his room. The cops hadn't been interested in either event. First they said that foreign visitors on short-term visas disappeared all the time and since Koshan's laptop had also gone missing, his departure had clearly been voluntary. ICE might want to find him but the Austin city police had better things to worry about.

You'd think the break-in would have changed their minds, but it worked the other way. *Because* Koshan had taken off of his own free will (they said) there was no reason to assume the break-in had anything to do with him. These old houses near campus got burglarized all the time, and I didn't even have anything missing.

Then Blossom invited me to visit for a week in the house she and Floss had rented in Port Aransas, Craig announced his intention of protecting me by moving into the spare room and my life, and I took off for the beach.

And now I had a total stranger clumping around my bathroom.

It was like that thing you do with dominos. I let an old friend talk me into renting a room to somebody I didn't know, and the dominos started falling, one after another.

Chaotically.

I don't like chaos; it fools you into doing things that are way too much trouble.

I had no idea, then, how far back the roots of that chaos went. Or how much more complexity and danger it was going to bring into my life.

2. The language of the dragon

The old German professor who was paying for this trek into the Pamirs was probably certifiably insane, but Koshan didn't mind. Guiding foreign trekkers paid a lot better than tutoring other students in English – the only other kind of work he'd been able to find since graduating with that shiny degree in psychology – and he hadn't had that many guiding jobs since the unpleasantness last fall. It hadn't been his fault that he and two of his trekkers were taken hostage by terrorists from that Religious Liberation Party. And despite their blood-curdling threats to bomb Lake Shaimak and flood half the country, nothing had actually happened, had it? The lake was still there. None of the hostages, even that American woman who kept trying to reason with their captors, had been harmed. And rumor said that the unstable mass of rocks that had been threatening the lake ever since the earthquake that created it was… gone. Crumbled into dust. Although nobody seemed to be quite sure how that had happened.

But his fellow Taklans were extremely sensitive on the topic of Lake Shaimak; it had been the scary dragon of their parents' stories for generations. And as a result, he discovered, even the slightest connection with the terrorists who'd threatened the lake made people revert to their infancy, when they'd been frightened into good behavior by the threat that "The Dragon of Shaimak will flood the whole world and drown you!" Most of the regular employees of Silk Road Treks didn't even like to be seen talking to Koshan these days.

So a rich foreigner who actually asked Silk Road Treks to find guides with experience in the Shaimak area was a gift from Allah.

All right, so Koshan hadn't actually been at the great lake when the Russians and Americans killed the terrorists before they could detonate their bomb. He, together with all but one of the other hostages, had been left at the village of Tireza, which wasn't even inside the Shaimak Restricted Area. But that was closer than anybody else had been, and he did have a distant relative whom he called "Auntie" in Tireza and even more distant connections whom he called "Cousin" in Shaimak itself... and the German paid extra for his inside knowledge.

Definitely a gift from Allah. He could get out of Mirzadeh, where there were too many people he owed money to after a lean winter and spring. And if he could spin out the trek past the planned month's duration, he might even come back with enough money to pay his creditors – well, the most urgent of them, anyway. It was a waste of money to pay *all* one's debts.

The drive up to Tireza in one of the comfortable jeeps belonging to Silk Road Treks was a vast improvement over his enforced journey of last fall, made partly in an unpressurized airplane and partly in the back of a dilapidated truck where he'd shared space with boxes of Semtex and wild-eyed terrorists who always seemed on the verge of shooting someone. The season was better, too. That last trip had been made in late October, when winter was just around the corner. The outside air had smelled like snow and the houses were smoky with burning yak dung. As a ragged boy in the Pamirs he'd taken the use of dung as fuel for granted, but the years in Merzadeh had taught him to think of that smoke as an unpleasant stench, the smell of poverty.

Now, in June, most of the snows that blocked access to the high valleys were gone. The air was fresh and green and even, at least in the sunshine, *warm*. Smiling girls came out at each village to offer them bread and salt, and between villages old Professor Teller bent Koshak's ear with his theories about the Shaimaki, Alexander the Great, precursor languages, and ancient religions. He had a notebook – an old-fashioned narrow bound ledger with a green cover – containing a few words in the old language that he thought only a few people in Shaimak village still spoke. It was not, he said authoritatively, related to Farsi or Taklan.

"It is like Greek?" Koshan said tentatively. He'd encountered this breed of professor in the past. The ones who came on treks liked to talk about Alexander the Great and how the fair-haired peasants in the Pamirs were probably descendants of his army. If every blond in Taklanistan was descended from someone in Alexander's army, Koshan was surprised the soldiers had had time to do any actual fighting.

Herr Professor Teller waved that suggestion away, shoo! Shoo! As though he were brushing that idea out of the window. No, old Shaimaki had no possible relationship to Greek; it was, he said, a much older language. As for Alexander, he had been a madman, a destroyer. He had smashed the people and their culture, had driven their last remnants to hide in these remote valleys. Rukshana, now, Alexander's supposedly Sogdian wife, had probably really been Shaimaki, the last high priestess of her people and the last who truly understood the secret power of the language...

Koshan mastered the art of nodding at intervals and emitting a thoughtful "Hmm," whenever the professor's spate of theorizing slowed. What he found much more interesting than these fantasies about ancient people was the ease with which they passed the guard posts protecting the Shaimak Restricted Area. Professor Teller must be very rich indeed, to have bribed enough people to get the four people and two jeeps comprising this trek into the area on a few days' notice. True, if the rocks called the Dragon of Shaimak had indeed crumbled as rumored, the integrity of the lake and its earthen dam were not menaced as they had been for the past hundred years. But requirements and permissions and passes did not change just because reality did; generations of government workers had made a good thing out of the bribes they took to let anyone past the boundaries, and they would probably still be requiring special passes and taking bribes a hundred years in the future.

This wasn't really a proper trek, even. The old German probably could not have hiked a mile at this altitude, and he didn't want to: all he wanted was somebody to shepherd him up to Shaimak village and to take care of all his material needs for the duration of the stay. This too was fine with Koshan. He had done enough high-country walking as a boy; he wouldn't mind if he never had to set foot out of a jeep again. Besides, even when he was sitting quietly in the jeep, Professor Teller's color and breathing were alarming. Koshan had suggested twice that they might stay a few days at one of the lower-altitude villages they went through, to allow Teller time to acclimatize. The professor had dismissed the suggestions with an irritable snap. His permissions for Shaimak had cleared and he wanted to get there with no further waste of time.

"It is not wasting time to take care of your health," Koshan had persisted the second time he tried to get the professor to slow down.

Teller gave him a sharp look. "You don't understand. You are young, you have years ahead of you. I do not *have* time. I have spent all I had and used all my reputation to make this trip happen. If I do not collect the information I need now, I may never have another chance. If my health is another casualty of the search for truth, so be it."

And when Koshan asked what kind of "truth" the professor expected to find in an isolated village of the High Pamirs, he got his ears filled with another hour of gobbledygook about glottochronology and missing linguistic links and the early migrations of Central Asian peoples. Mixed in with that was a bunch of nonsense about the reports of last October's events, which had evidently been what captured the professor's interest. The reports he liked best were the sensational garbage from the tabloid press, from writers who apparently didn't understand that the "dragon of Shaimak," wasn't an actual dragon but just a colorful way of describing the unstable rock mass that threatened the lake.

For the most part, even Professor Teller didn't seem to care about what he was saying: it was just words, words being spouted out the way some marine animals squirted out clouds of ink to disguise themselves.

But what could an elderly German academic, a man who by his own admission had never before left the comfort of the university libraries to conduct research in the field, have to hide? Koshan couldn't imagine.

When they camped below Shaimak, on the last night of the journey, he asked the other two Silk Road employees if they had any idea what the German hoped to find in Shaimak. "Rubies?" suggested Farzad, who had loaded up the other jeep with spices, dehydrated food and other supplies that he turned into a hot meal for them every night.

Naraiman, driver of the other jeep and keeper of the maps and permits, shook his head. "The mines were closed over a hundred years ago! Every ruby they produced must have been traded out of here for food long since."

"I did hear they had re-opened the mines," Farzad persisted. "Now that the Dragon of Shaimak is crumbled into rubble – isn't that right, Koshan? You were here, weren't you?"

Koshan shook his head unwillingly. "I was down in Tireza when all that happened." He didn't like to admit his ignorance, since his supposed expertise in the Shaimak area had been what got him this job. But there was no point in lying to his fellows. It would be too easy for them to catch him out.

"Even so," said Naraiman, "there never were enough rubies to make this area worth developing. And I can't believe that the last half-year has been so productive that a rich man from Germany would expect to get a profit from this little mine!"

In the morning, when Koshan took his place in the driver's seat of the lead jeep and started the grinding climb up to Shaimak village – the "new" village that was only a hundred years old, not the original one that had been slowly drowned when Lake Shaimak started to fill up after the earthquake – Professor Teller looked sideways at him and chuckled. "You boys were – trying to find out – what riches the old fool is chasing, eh?" He let go a series of breathy laughs broken by gasps.

"We did wonder," Koshan said.

"I know. Rubies, eh? *La'al?*"

Koshan glanced at him, surprised.

"I know a few words of Taklan," Professor Teller said.

"But—" The boss at Silk Road had told Koshan he was being hired as a guide and interpreter.

"I do not plan to waste my time learning enough Taklan to negotiate with the locals," Teller said impatiently. "Don't be concerned, you will – earn – your fee."

Koshan would have felt more secure about that if the old man hadn't started gasping and coughing again.

When they got their permits, back in Merzadeh, a member of the patrol guarding the Lake Shaimak Restricted Area had driven up to Shaimak to tell the villagers of the honor they were about to receive, whether they wanted it or not. At the outskirts of the village, therefore, they were greeted by brightly dressed girls carrying baskets of bread and salt. Koshan saw one familiar face and waved discreetly. Rukshana returned his signal with a beaming smile and a broad, totally indiscreet wave. One of the older girls elbowed her; he suspected another lecture on proper behavior was in his little cousin's future. Not that it would bother Rukshana! When she'd stayed with their aunt to attend the village school in Tireza, she'd attracted disapproving lectures the way other girls attracted young men.

On the day of their arrival Teller was too exhausted by the trip to be much of a nuisance. He let Koshan blow up an air mattress and set up a collapsible table and chair for him in the house that the villagers had made available, ate the meal that Farzad produced to go with the freshly baked rounds of local bread, and went to sleep with his battered German copy of *Faust* spread open on his chest.

On the next day, though, the rest seemed to have given him a new lease of life. He wasn't even gasping and coughing the way he'd done on the way up to Shaimak. Perhaps he was acclimatizing after all! He certainly had enough energy to be a nuisance. First he pointed out the four rows of successively smaller wooden beams rising up to the skylight above the roof and told Koshan that the number four went back to Zoroastrian times. "The first beam stands for the earth, the second water, the next fire and the highest air —that is, the four basic elements."

That might be true, but since every Pamiri house had exactly that structure, Koshan didn't think it proved much about the survivals of ancient folkways among these particular villagers. And the rest of the central room looked just like any other house in any other village, except smaller and shabbier. The layers of felt mats covering the floor were thin and the colors faded, and only a few wooden bowls and dishes were stored in the wall frames. The ragged pieces of patchwork hung here and there on the walls were threadbare and faded, and had never been embroidered. There was not even a copper pitcher for serving water.

After examining the house, Professor Teller began to exercise his full potential as a pest to the whole village. He elbowed his way in among the women when they were kneading the day's bread, pointing at the bowl they kneaded in, the oven outside the front door, the carved wooden chests where they kept their clothes, and asking – asking – asking about everything. He bothered the men and women working on their vegetable plots, pointing at plants and clods of dirt and wooden hoes and repeating what they said into his little recording device. There wasn't a thing he left unquestioned, from the patties of yak dung drying on the tops of stone walls to the patient yaks themselves.

And at the end of the day he sat over his recorder, playing back his collection of words with a disappointed look. "Angusht," he said. "Aingus. Gusht…"

Koshan's lips twitched, just before Teller himself figured it out. *"Himmelherrgott,"* the German howled, "I have collected seventy times seven ways to say 'finger!'" His eyes met Koshan's and after a moment of pure rage, he began laughing. "Tell me, boy. What should I have done instead of pointing at things?"

"We, um, we mostly point with our chins. Like this," Koshan said, jerking his own chin towards the door. "It's, um, not really *polite* to jab at things with your finger."

"So your people decided to give the old man a little lesson in courtesy." Teller was sticking to his good-humored tone with some effort. "Very well, very well. Even the few words they have given me are of no use; they are merely a rural dialect of Taklan."

"That is what we speak," Koshan pointed out.

"But it's no good to me!" Teller raised his hand as if to dash the little recorder onto the floor, then stopped himself. "I want to learn the *old* language."

Old, he wanted? Very well; on the next day Koshan dragged the oldest man in the village to meet his client. That man listened, nodded, shook his head, and finally gave Teller a few words that sounded like nothing Koshan had ever heard. If dragons existed and had a language, he thought, this is what their speech would sound like: words full of the clashing of rocks, hissing with blue flame.

Over the next few days Teller became somewhat less of a nuisance to the village as a whole – that is, he was only a nuisance to one person at a time, leaving the others free to get on with their work. It did not seem to Koshan that he was getting much of this "old language" from any one person, but the recordings slowly mounted up. At night, after the communal meal, Teller would sit at his flimsy desk and replay his day's collection, scribbling as he did so in the narrow ledger with the stained green cover. Koshan contrived to get a glimpse of the writing but was left no wiser than before: it was some kind of spiky script that he couldn't begin to read.

A spiky script for a stony language?

One day a villager interrupted their preparation of dinner to say that the professor wanted an interpreter. Koshan followed the man and found Teller pestering Rukshana. That was odd; Rukshana was one of the few people in the village who'd been sent to Tireza every summer to attend the seasonal school there. The school didn't teach German, but if anybody knew enough English to communicate with Professor Teller, she should.

He had the feeling she didn't want to communicate with Teller. He told Koshan that he needed to know *exactly* what she had said just before something or other had happened.

"Nothing happened! The wool is clean now, that is all," she snapped. She put aside the sieve on which she'd rested a bundle of wool while tweaking the horsehair string tied across the sieve to beat dust out of the bundle.

"But she barely touched it," Teller complained.

Koshan took a pinch of the wool between finger and thumb, raised it and blew on the fibers. "If you can get all the dust and dirt out so quickly, Rukshana, you should clean the wool for the whole village!"

"The old man is mistaken," she told him, flushing. "I had to work a long time to clean this much!"

"*Nein!* She did not," said Teller.

"And now," Rukshana said, "I must begin cleaning another batch." She put the clean wool in a large bowl, pulled dirty wool out of the sack beside her and arranged it on the sieve, under the taut horsehair string.

"And then she said, '*Djnd vlaad dzlaamk!*'" It was Teller who voiced the grating words.

Dust and loose dirt cascaded from the sieve, and Rukhshana's fingers were only just raised to pluck the string. White-faced, she turned to the professor, and then to Koshan. "I did not say it," she cried out. "I never said it, I do not know where he learned it! I never used it to clean the wool – well, only a little, little bit, and my fingers are so sore!" Tearful, she exhibited pink fingertips to Koshan. "Please do not tell anyone!"

"Do not tell them what?"

"That I used the language of the dragon to clean my wool."

3. A Faustian bargain

"The language of the dragon!" The old man was so excited that he started gasping and coughing again.

"Please, sit down and rest," Koshan begged him. "You will kill yourself if you go on like this." Teller had come back from Rukshana's to prance around the house, pointing at things and trying out more sentences that sounded like rockfalls… and then laughing, whooping, and scribbling furiously in that ledger of his.

"*Bin ich ein Gott?* Am I a God?" he chanted, waving his copy of *Faust*. "In these pure symbols do I see / Nature exert her energy!"

And that was just the part of his activities that Koshan could stand to think about.

"You need to sit down," he urged Teller again when he saw the professor rubbing his head. Headache was one of the signs of altitude sickness, and all this pointing and shouting wasn't going to help. "Altitude sickness can kill you." Maybe if he said it often enough, the warning would sink in.

"Ah, who cares about an old man's life?"

Koshan had found that the professor wasn't moved by assertions of empathy. "If you die, they may not pay us for the whole trek, and I need the money."

"Ach, money! We shall be rich, you fool! This discovery is worth more than life itself. When I publish, it will make me immortal!" The professor pointed at a brass samovar whose incised surface had grown dingy with neglect. "*Samovar vlaad dzlaamk!*" he shouted.

Much to Koshan's relief, nothing happened. That hadn't always been the case since their return from Rukshana's home.

"The wrong word," Professor Teller groaned. "Boy, I need to know how to say 'samovar' in Alt-Shaimaki. No, I do not," he contradicted himself immediately. "'Samovar' is a Russian loan-word in Taklan; the old ones would have had no word for the thing. I need to learn words for what is always with us. Earth, stones, water, snow…"

"Alt-Shaimaki?" Koshan asked.

"Ahh, in English you would say Old Shaimaki. But a *German* has discovered the secret of the language, not an American or Briton, and so it will be Alt-Shaimaki when I publish. *Teller's* Alt-Shaimaki, they will say!" And the old man demanded Koshan's arm to support him back outside, so that he could collect more words to play with.

"My little cousin called it 'the language of the dragon.'"

Teller cackled and shot Koshan a bright, measuring glance. "So she did – she did! It is a metaphor, of course; this is the language of *power*. Who speaks Alt-Shaimaki will have power like a dragon – dragons…" His eyes clouded over. "What about dragons? Who are you?" he demanded. "Are you trying to steal my results?"

Koshan introduced himself all over again and reminded Teller that he'd been hired as a guide and interpreter. "I know that," the professor said impatiently. "Ask that boy how to say 'stone' in the old language."

The boy was a few years younger than Rukshana. He shook his head and said, "I am too young to speak with dragons. You will have to ask an elder."

The first three men Koshan and Teller approached also shook their heads, frowning. The fourth said, "Why do you need to call *tsh*?" and then backed away, looking unhappy.

"*Tsh*," Teller repeated for the recorder on his way back to the house.

"*Tsh*," he said again indoors as he scribbled in the notebook that he never showed to anyone. "Faust, Faust, be you my guide!" he cried. "As the student said to Mephistopheles, '*Was man schwarz auf weiß besitzt / Kann man getrost nach Hause tragen.* What we possess in black and white, / We can in peace and comfort bear away!'"

Back at the door, he stooped and picked up a pebble and leaned on Koshan to get upright again.

"Tsh vlaad dzlaamk!" he cried out, and minute crumbs of dirt fell from his hand, leaving only the bare rock, as clean as if it had been washed in a basin and dried with a guest towel.

"I can do anything!" Teller cackled. "I am a great man! I, I shall…" He paused for a moment, frowning as if he was having trouble remembering something. "I shall *publish*. Yes. That is what we call it."

The four older men, the three who hadn't spoken and the one who had let the word for 'stone' slip, approached the door. "What does he plan?"

Koshan did his best to explain scholarly journals and publications in the village Taklan.

"He will give the language of the dragon to strangers?"

"It will be written for anybody to read?"

"We cannot permit this," said the oldest of the four.

"Ha! You cannot stop me! Nobody can stop me!" Teller laughed when Koshan translated their concerns. He held out his hand with the clean rock in it, and said, *"Tsh vlaad… vlaad…* ah, yes. *Tsh vlaad kzmtq!"* He giggled like a child as they all stared at his empty palm. "I did that…" A lost look crossed his features. "Did I do that? My head aches so…" He rubbed his eyes.

"You dropped your little rock," Koshan said firmly. "You need to rest now."

The professor looked blank and confused.

"It begins," said the oldest man.

"What did you do to him?"

"He is doing it to himself."

They followed Teller and Koshan back to the house they were using, and watched while Koshan persuaded the professor to lie down for a rest. When he stood, the oldest man extended one hand. "You will give us the talking-machine."

"I don't know what you mean," Koshan parried.

The other three men moved in and held him with surprising strength for such ancient villagers, while Zardusht the headman knelt beside Teller and picked up the recorder.

"Is this Pamiri hospitality?" Koshan demanded, struggling in vain against the arms that restrained him. "Grandfather, uncles, do you steal from guests? You make me ashamed to be Pamiri!"

"This guest sought to steal from us," the headman said. "I am sorry about his device, but in the city he will doubtless be able to buy another talking-machine." Stepping outside, he dropped the recorder on a rock and pressed his boot on it. The flexible yak-hide sole did little damage. He picked up a stone somewhat larger than the one that had... *not*... disappeared from Professor Teller's palm, and brought it down on the recorder once, twice, three times. "*Bu prdmt vlaad kzmtq!*"

The shattered bits of metal and plastic were no longer there.

They left Koshan with the professor then. Farhad and Naraiman had announced their intention of accepting an invitation to the mid-day meal from a large family boasting several marriageable girls, so he was alone to deal with a man whose insanity grew by the minute. As soon as the Pamiris left them, Teller demanded his notebook in a hoarse whisper. "They don't know about the notebook. Don't tell them! 'What we possess in black and white...'" He scribbled for several minutes before falling back against his pillows, pen in hand. "*Bu prdmt vlaad kzmtq!*" he gasped. The pen vanished and Teller cackled. "But not the notebook, no, not the notebook," he said. A sly smile crossed his face and he scrabbled for the narrow ledger with its green cover. Koshan put it into his hand and he slid it under the pillow.

By the time Farhad and Naraiman returned several more small objects had vanished from the house. Teller seemed less rational with each use of the language he called Alt-Shaimaki, and by early evening he had subsided into insane mutterings. Koshan decided that the man was suffering from the cerebral edema that sometimes accompanied altitude sickness. He decided not to think about the fact that Teller had appeared to be acclimatizing, and he definitely did not wish to think about wool that cleaned itself and rocks and recorders that disappeared themselves.

But in the morning, when they found Teller dead, Koshan managed to slip that notebook in with his own possessions before they packed up the professor's body and belongings for return to the city.

4. This thing disappears

Merzadeh was not a friendly city for Koshan that summer. As he had gloomily predicted, Silk Road Treks paid him and the other two guides only for the days they had actually been on the road, not for the full month the professor had requested. What he received was hardly enough to placate his creditors, and it seemed foolish to try once he found out that the old witch who rented him a room had sold his laptop to cover the unpaid rent. The cost of replacing the laptop made a nasty hole in the payment from Silk Road, but what was a man to do? He couldn't maintain a civilized life, keep up with his friends, follow the news or play at the new gaming sites without a computer! Besides, a few lucky days of gaming and he would be...

Even less able to pay his debts than when he'd left Merzadeh for the High Pamirs.

Gloomily, Koshan considered his remaining assets. Good snowshoes, down pants and jackets, other cold-weather gear would fetch him far less than the price he'd paid for those items. And without his own gear, his chance of picking up occasional guiding jobs would shrink to almost nothing. He would sell the new laptop before he sold his trekking gear – and he was *not* going to sell the new laptop.

Only one thing remained: that small notebook filled with the illegible, spiky script of the old professor. Teller had thought the notebook would make him rich and famous. It ought to be worth something... to the right person. But how was he going to find that person?

It would have to be somebody at a university. And not the University of

Merzadeh, where the study of Taklan traditions was considered vastly inferior to important subjects like highway engineering and industrial psychology. No, he needed a foreigner, from a foreign university, with the vast sums of money all those people threw around when they visited Taklanistan.

He did know one American with university connections. Better yet, he had been nice to her when they'd been held hostage by those terrorists last fall; she might feel some good will towards him still. And during the time they spent together she had made it clear that her alma mater, the University of Texas at Austin, was the finest university in the United States, to which better-known institutions such as Harvard and Princeton were like butter-lamps to an electric light. So Koshan felt quite confident that he was contacting the right person when he sent an email to Thalia Lensky, including some scans of notebook pages, to ask how he could turn this information into money.

Thalia's reply was instant, warm-hearted, and – initially – disappointing. She couldn't read the notebook pages any better than he could, and she had no idea to whom he could send them.

With her second paragraph, things began to look up. He'd mentioned a recent trek to Shaimak? After several foolish feminine questions about Rukshana and other unimportant people in the village, she got to the point. Every July, the university hosted a conference on Central Asian Languages and Cultures. Could he possibly attend the upcoming conference? There he was sure to find people who could interpret the notes and tell him what they were worth.

Koshan wrote back lamenting the poverty that made a transatlantic journey impossible for him. Americans were rich; maybe she would send him a ticket.

She didn't do that, but she did find a way to get him invited to the conference as a speaker, which meant that his way would be paid. She commented that people seemed to be quite interested in hearing from someone who was actually familiar with the remote, fabled region of Shaimak. Somebody had even asked her if it was true that the villagers still practiced Zoroastrianism. Of course she couldn't speak to such matters, but if Koshan could…

Koshan decided on the spot that if the Americans wanted the Shaimak villagers to be Zoroastrians, they would *be* Zoroastrians. He could tell them what Teller had said about the skylight construction without mentioning that every single Pamiri village used the same structure. To add to that he did some quick Web research, was relieved to find that the religion was mostly about fire worship with no icky stuff about human sacrifice, and sent off an abstract that got him the desired formal invitation. It didn't actually pay money, but at least his fare to and from the conference would be covered.

He could probably get a refund on the return portion of the ticket and use that to cover his expenses until he located an American who would make him rich in return for the contents of the notebook.

Thalia's good will extended to finding Koshan an inexpensive place to stay during the conference, a vacant room in the house of some woman who'd tutored her in French and who only accepted him as a short-term tenant on Thalia's enthusiastic recommendation.

It had been a good day for Koshan when he persuaded the terrorists to let Thalia scrounge up some warm clothes from the villagers at Tireza before they dragged her up to the heights of New Shaimak. She must have mentioned that warm outfit half a dozen times in the few minutes she spent introducing him to this Sienna Brown. Getting the impression that he had literally saved her friend's life, Sienna Brown was almost as favorably inclined to him as Thalia herself. The only thing that confused him was why she wanted to rent out a room. Anybody who possessed such a fine house, with stucco walls and glass windows, with four bedrooms and *two* indoor bathrooms, with floors of real wood and furniture instead of cushions, must be even richer than most Americans. There was even a separate room for cooking pots and utensils!

Not that it mattered much, once he was *there*. Thalia Lensky was no longer the little, quick-moving woman he had rather admired last fall: she was extremely pregnant, far past the stage at which a decent Taklan woman would keep to her house instead of forcing men to look at her swollen body. She and Sienna wasted his time jabbering about heat and the discomforts of pregnancy until he could only be grateful when she left saying that she might not be back; it was *so* hot, she thought she would not leave the comfort of her own air-conditioned home again until it was time to go to the hospital.

As for his new landlady, she seemed to think a lot of her own linguistic abilities, but Koshan was not that impressed. She had tutored Thalia in French, and she mentioned a handful of other languages, but none of them were any use: why should he care that she knew German and Spanish? She didn't speak Taklan or any of the neighboring languages like Kyrgyz or Uzbek. He didn't waste his time asking her about the notebook pages; he stuffed the notebook itself under his mattress and went off to the conference, computer under his arm, to act the expert on Shaimak and, hopefully, to meet a real expert who would see the potential in the scanned images on the laptop.

He did have one name now, thanks to this Sienna Brown. She'd told him that the expert on Central Asia in the linguistics department was a tenured professor named Edward Osborne. He was not, she said, an easy man to approach, but his scholarship was amazing.

"You could introduce me?"

Sienna shook her head. "I was just one of a hundred undergraduates in his survey course. The T.A. might remember me, but not Dr. Osborne. In any case, given his attitude towards undergraduates you might be better off without my introduction. He felt that teaching us was an intolerable imposition on his time; all he really cared about was giving a couple of advanced seminars for his dissertation candidates."

But since the person Koshan actually got to talk to was one of the teaching assistants, Sienna's name did him some good.

"Oh, *Sienna!*" Mira Martinez said happily. "No, I wasn't one of Dr. Osborne's T.A.'s then, I was just an undergraduate, but we had Russian together. Everybody around here knows Sienna! Crazy girl, she used to go through language classes like Michael Moore would go through a hotel buffet. If she thinks your papers are something Dr. Osborne would be interested in, you can leave them with me. I'll make sure he takes a look at them."

On the way to the campus, Koshan had stopped at an Internet café to print out just one of his three scanned pages from the notebook. Now he took that printout, tore it in half, scribbled his new phone number on one piece and gave it to the teaching assistant. He had no intention of being conned into giving away too much; if these notes were as valuable as the old German had claimed, this would be enough of a sample to whet the professor's interest.

He still hadn't heard from Osborne three days later, when it was time for him to give his scheduled talk, "Remnants of Zoroastrianism and Mazdayasna in the High Pamirs." He'd had ample time to do his research by then, and he felt proud of his speech. Describing the position of Shaimak, overlooking the Lake of the Dragon and cut off from the world for months at a time behind snowed-in passes, required only telling what was actually so. Even his description of village life was mostly straightforward: the grinding poverty, the trade-offs between using yak dung as fertilizer for the crops or as fuel to keep the people from freezing, the long winter nights of storytelling and singing. Then his imagination took over and he described the sacred cord given to children when they reached the age of reason and could be initiated into the secret cult, the temple where the sacred fire must be kept constantly alive, the solemnization of marriage by the couple's jumping hand in hand over the fire... The more details he pulled out of his recent reading, the happier the audience seemed to be. By the end of the talk nearly all of them were scribbling notes or recording his speech on their phones.

It was a good thing that Shaimak really was so isolated, Koshan thought. His little cousin Rukshana would never stop teasing him if she could hear the farrago of dreams and fantasies he'd fed to this crowd.

He had some trouble extricating himself from the people who wanted to ask questions, but after about half an hour one of the conference organizers whisked him away to a quiet back room, thanked him for his contributions to scholarship, and left him to recollect himself in peace.

Well, almost in peace. The aide's last words were, "... someone who shares your deep knowledge of and interest in Pamiri life," and when he left the room, a middle-aged man with a deeply creased, weatherbeaten face entered. "Mighty interesting presentation, son," the man drawled. He introduced himself as Hank Henderson – "just plain Hank, I don't have any academic initials to put before or after my name" – and followed up his initial compliment by affably informing Koshan that his presentation had been one of the finest examples of creative bullshit he had been privileged to hear.

"I don't know what you are talking about," Koshan said, and then, recognizing a better line of defense, "and I think *you* do not know what you are talking about either! I am Pamiri—"

"But not Shaimaki, eh, son? Come on, now, you got the material for that very imaginative talk off the Internet. Half of it was lifted straight from the Occult Arts of Asia website, I recognized the wording."

Koshan shook his head. "Well, it don't matter," Hank said cheerfully. "I *was* just a tad interested when I heard somebody from Shaimak was speaking here, but all that's been lost is a little bit of my time. Too bad you don't actually know anything about Shaimak, or I might have made it worth your while to help me out here."

"Maybe I know more than you think!" Koshan riposted. "Do you know any of…" What had Teller called it? "Of the *old* language of Shaimak?"

Hank's grey eyes blazed with sudden light. "Do *you*? Or is this just another line of BS?"

Koshan took a ballpoint pen out of his pocket and balanced it on his open hand. He'd show this nobody who he was talking to! "*Bu prdmt vlaad kzmtq!*"

Hank applauded, gently clapping his hands together. "So you do magic tricks as well?"

All this – something or other – was giving Koshan a headache and making it hard to concentrate. Why shouldn't he just make Hank disappear? Oh, right, the man had hinted that he had money.

"I think you know it is not a trick," he said. "How much is it worth to you?"

"One sentence, one little trick? Not much," Hank said.

Koshan pulled the remaining scrap of his printed scan out of his pocket and showed it to the American. While Hank was studying it Koshan's phone buzzed, and he glanced at the screen. Osborne! "Think it over," he told Hank. "Maybe I will get back to you." And maybe not, if this Dr. Osborne was prepared to be generous.

Edward Osborne scowled at the impudent young man who was trying to sell him – him! – Paul Teller's research on Alt-Shaimaki. "Scholarship, young man, is not to be bought and sold in the marketplace. You should be ashamed of trying to profit from Professor Teller's work."

"*He* thought to profit from it," the man insisted. "He said we would be rich!"

Osborne laughed gently. "You misunderstood. Teller was a scholar; he meant that this work would make him famous. That is the only wealth that matters among those of us who devote our lives to the search for truth."

"Then I suppose the question is, how much is fame worth to you?"

Osborne glanced at the door to his office. The lights in the outer office were out. Before this Koshan Idrisov arrived, he had told his secretary that she could take the rest of the day off. If he did get forced into paying for data, well, that wasn't something he'd want to have generally known. But surely he could get the information out of this kid without going that far!

"No, the question is, what can you actually deliver?" He tapped the crumpled half-sheet printout on his desk. "A few phrases – so far, what you have to offer is not impressive."

"You can read it?"

"German script," Osborne said off-handedly. Good point, that, and one that was on his side of the argument. "Most Americans cannot read German script. Your 'valuable information' would be no more than some spiky scribbling to my compatriots. I am afraid, Mr. Idrisov, that I am the only possible customer for your information. And as you must know, when there is but one buyer, he sets the price."

"There might be others."

"Then I suggest you speak to them."

"You have no use for the paper I gave you?"

"None," Osborn lied. It wasn't even much of a lie; as soon as he had transcribed the handful of phrases on the printout, he would destroy the paper."

Idrisov's eyes narrowed. "*Bu prdmt vlaad kzmtq!*"

The paper vanished from between Osborne's fingers; he could almost feel its molecules floating free into the air.

"You destructive fool!" He jumped up from his desk and grabbed Idrisov by the shoulders. "Do you have *any idea* of the value of this material? You idiot!" Idrisov was young, but Osborne was tall and powerfully built; he shook Idrisov and pushed him away in one furious move. The Taklan seemed to be dizzy. Instead of resisting he put one hand to his head, staggered, and fell to his knees. His head hit the corner of the desk with a terrible crack.

And then he stopped moving.

Panting, Osborne stared down at the body of the younger man. It hadn't happened. None of this had happened. He was dreaming. In a minute he would come back to reality. He would still be holding that fragment of a page with words in Alt-Shaimaki, and this greedy little Taklan would still be trying to make him set a price on priceless knowledge.

But there was no sound in the office louder than the blood rushing through his head, and the Taklan guide, lying in a loose-limbed sprawl that bent his body unnaturally, did not move.

Very slowly, Osborne picked up the laptop that Koshan Idrisov had brought with him and placed it in a bottom desk drawer. When he called the campus police and explained the terrible accident, there would be no need to mention that little detail.

But – perhaps he need not do even that. He did have a good memory for languages; the one thing Idrisov had said in Alt-Shaimaki still rang clear in his mind. It was ridiculous, of course, to think that what made a piece of paper vanish would work on something as large as a body – but – no harm in trying?

Fighting revulsion, he knelt beside Koshan's body and reached into a pocket to get his phone. He didn't know where the paper had gone, but if he *did* manage to send the body to the same place, he didn't want the phone, with its record of his call, to go with it. He needed to keep control of that incriminating thing.

He stood, stashed the phone with the laptop, and pointed at the body. "*Bu prdmt vlaad kzmtq.*"

He had a *really terrible* blinding migraine.

But he also had an empty office again.

5. The girl is scared stiff

My first stop the next morning was at Sweet Georgia Realty. The office occupied the bottom half of my aunt's house on Rio Grande; a pleasant set of rooms, with oak floors, high ceilings and old-fashioned sash windows (and slightly less pleasant old-fashioned window air conditioners; it hadn't been retrofitted for central air like my parents' house). Aunt Georgia and I were both "rich" in inherited houses, although she had a better work ethic and hence, less of a perennial crisis with the property taxes.

I had a courtesy desk in the main room, though the other two realtors who worked in there had a bad habit of using it as a place to stash their paperwork. It was too much trouble to bug them about it; it wasn't like I ever expected to spend much time actually sitting at the desk.

It was a pleasant room, large enough for us to arrange our desks in a semicircle, with oak floors that glowed in the summer sunshine that slanted through the tall windows. And my colleagues were decorative too, in their own ways: Davis with broad shoulders and a pleasant face, Carly with dark curly hair like Laura's and a piquant little face accented with eye shadow and bright red lipstick. For once, both of them were in the office, not out showing places. Must be a slow period.

Davis, as usual in August, was dressed in what I thought of as Midsummer Respectable: slacks and shirt of the lightest-weight fabric known to humanity. I sometimes wondered if they'd dissolve during one of our infrequent summer downpours. Could be interesting to observe.

Carly, who was tiny and compact, was doing Professional Realtor (Edgy

Modern) in a red jacket over a navy dress, stacked red heels and pantyhose. The kind of look I sometimes aspired to but rarely achieved in an Austin summer. Pantyhose and hundred-degree days don't mix well. Unless, like Carly, you had ice water in your... Oops. I'd resolved to cut down on the uncharitable asides. Even if I didn't say the words out loud, I had a theory that thinking them generated aggressive vibes that made my working relationship with Carly edgier than it had to be, and not in a fashion-forward sense.

Davis gave me a friendly nod and gestured towards one of the stacks of papers on my desk.

"That's okay, I can work around it," I responded to the unspoken offer to move his stuff. It would just add another little source of tension if Davis cleared his papers off my desk and Carly didn't remove hers – and Carly was sitting back with her arms folded, giving me the evil eye. Clearly not about to give back any of the space she'd appropriated. Oh well, I was only there to discuss the new rental with Aunt Georgia.

"I thought you'd be glad of the money," my aunt said when I followed her into her office to grumble about this surprise rental. "You certainly complained enough about finances after your old tenant moved to California –"

"Colorado."

"Whatever. And then you said that foreign boy Thalia recommended took off without paying the rest of the rent he owed you?"

"I should never have let him talk me into giving him a key before I had the cash. I've been having so much trouble around that room, I was thinking of making it into part of a private suite for myself instead of renting it out again." I fiddled with one of the curls trying to break loose from the scrunchie that held them out of my face. Austin shouldn't have been more humid than the *beach*, but my hair was acting as if it had been power-frizzed.

"And how would you afford that?"

"Maybe I could make up the money doing a little more here at the office."

"I thought you'd never ask," Aunt Georgia said, and handed me three shiny new folders.

"But now that I'm getting rent for that room again..."

"Don't be silly, it's high time you grew up and started doing a responsible job instead of eking out a meagre existence by renting rooms in your parents' house. You can start today, with the top folder. The Stevensons specifically asked for you, God only knows why, and they've been waiting for you to get back from the beach."

Carly's evil-eye glare only intensified when I emerged from Aunt Georgia's office with the new paperwork, and she made a barely audible comment about how nice it must be to have an in with the boss.

It wasn't favoritism, not really. I'd been tutoring desperate language students since my freshman year at the university – that made what? Eight? No, nine years of making contacts with people, many of whom stayed in Austin after graduating and remembered me fondly. I wasn't just good at learning languages; I was also good at helping jittery students absorb the cruel realities of life, such as that French *les* is not pronounced "less" and that some German verbs can come apart like Legos to occupy distant parts of a sentence. Blossom and Floss regarded me as the sole buffer between them and ignominious expulsion from the Spanish Education program, and they weren't far wrong.

I'd tried to explain this fact of life to Carly before, but had never yet succeeded in communicating to her that the clients that she thought were just a gift from my aunt were actually the result of my having been in town a long time and having had the chance to help a lot of people. She went to business luncheon meetings, dressed for success, and had a huge profile on LinkedIn; she felt that I must be cheating somehow, to have clients without playing the networking game.

Now I took a quick look through the folders in my hand. Bruce and Angie Stevenson, I was definitely keeping those; they were the ones who'd made a point of waiting for me to get back so I could show them the Harris mansion on the lake. Next were a newly married couple, first-time home buyers, one of whom I had hand-carried through the pitfalls of Russian 201. Forget those, Carly wouldn't thank me for clients who would require lengthy education in the realities of real estate before settling for the kind of starter home they could get a mortgage on. The third client was a young man who'd demanded a crash course in Arabic so that he could be eligible for an overseas assignment with his company. The fact that he was back in Austin and shopping for a condo suggested the Arabic hadn't done the trick for him. He'd probably only contacted Sweet Georgia Realty because I was the only realtor he'd ever met.

I handed Carly his folder. "Would you do me a huge favor and take care of this one?" Maybe that would sweeten her temper.

Davis followed me out to the coffee and tea stand that occupied what had once been a front hall. "Sienna, you don't have to give in to Carly every time she grumbles. She knows just as well as I do why you have so many clients without hustling for them."

I sighed and searched through the tea bags for something that wasn't Earl Grey or Lapsang Souchong. "I know, but… well, it's not like I can take care of all three clients immediately. Somebody's going to have to wait or go with a different realtor, and if Carly takes them over, at least the business stays in the office." There was one bag of Orange Spice left. I poured hot water over it and jiggled it up and down by the string.

"If you hadn't been out of touch for a week…"

"Well, I was. It's a little late to fix that now!"

Davis' face shocked me and I apologized. "Sorry. Sorry. I didn't mean to snap." Too late I remembered Aunt Georgia's training: count to three before speaking, she always told me, and I wouldn't irritate so many people.

Fortunately, Davis was too sweet to stay irritated. He cheered up immediately, and I let him advise me on how to build my client list into a solid career while the tea steeped. It wasn't too hard; I let my eyes drift slightly out of focus, nodded at intervals, and developed my mini-fantasy about his shirt and slacks dissolving in a thunderstorm. That wouldn't display any more of his body than he showed on the tennis court three times a week, but the setting was more fun to daydream about. The hard-hitting tennis he played, that kept him in such good shape, also made him hot and sweaty and as close to aggressive and snarly as he ever got. Rain, on the other hand…

Well, rain was clearly not on the agenda today, and neither were fantasies. I had clients to appease. I contacted the Stevensons and was able to set up an appointment with them almost immediately. If that worked out, and if I was a very good girl and spent the long hours that would be necessary to talk Mr. and Mrs. Newlywed down to a starter home within their budget, and if Carly got somewhere with Mr. Executive Arabic, the clients would be happy; Aunt Georgia would be happy; possibly even Carly would be happy.

Life was a lot less trouble if people weren't annoyed with me. I really should appreciate Davis more; he coupled smooth good looks with reliable friendship and always accepted my apologies when I snapped at him. Too bad the real man didn't do as much for me as soaking-wet fantasy-Davis did. He was definitely a low-maintenance friend, and a girl could always use one of those.

A serious realtor, I knew, would regard clients like mine as a gift from God, not as a nuisance. The fact was that I'd never been all that serious about the real estate business. Getting my license had been less trouble than withstanding Aunt Georgia's insistence that having graduated from UT with a useless degree in linguistics, I really needed to get some kind of professional certification. And since then, okay, I'd closed just enough deals to keep me around the office on a semi-regular basis. It just wasn't *me*.

But then... I wasn't entirely sure what *was* me. My only real talent was a knack for picking up languages quickly, something I'd discovered in high school. And experience had demonstrated that a degree in linguistics bolstered by fluency in half a dozen languages and a smattering of a couple of dozen more would not quite buy me a latte at Starbucks. So, given property taxes and the cost of groceries and other unpleasant realities, I had better continue to do what Aunt Georgia suggested.

Out to the lake it was, then, to let myself into a conglomeration of glass and metal cubes and redwood decks that only somebody really, really rich could love. The place had a checkered history. The original builder hadn't been able to pay for his creation, and it had passed into the hands of one of *those* Harrises, the grocery store moguls. But the Whitney Harris who'd owned it for a few years had been involved in some kind of scandal – I hadn't paid attention to the details – and it was up for sale to pay her legal bills.

Had been up for sale for quite some time, actually, and the asking price had just been cut again. The kind of history realtors mean when we say,

"Motivated seller." No wonder the Stevensons were unhappy that I'd been out of town last week; they must have been afraid that someone else would snap up this unique house at the newly lowered price. Most people would have let another realtor show them the place. Wasn't it a good thing that Bruce Stevenson had been one of my first tutoring jobs when I started at UT? And that he was still so grateful to me for getting him past the German proficiency exams for his Ph.D. qualification?

For people who'd insisted they wanted me and nobody else to show them the lakeside property, Angie and Bruce Stevenson were awfully late. But considering that the commission I'd make on a house this size would make me feel financially independent for months, I could afford to wait on their convenience.

I got a respectable number of loyal clients like this every year, ex-students or referrals from ex-students like Thalia who thought that without me they'd never have passed their language requirements. In many cases they were right. And there was a certain karmic balance to the situation that I appreciated, because without them I wouldn't have any income at all from the real estate business. Aunt Georgia was constantly on my case to take the job more seriously, but as long as I could eat regularly and pay the sky-high property taxes on my house every year, it just didn't seem worth the trouble. Okay, I admit it: I'm an Austin slacker. Blue skies and a string of lakes like jewels, good Mexican food and a great live music scene keep our species alive with remarkably little cash flowing anywhere at all.

Certainly it was no hardship to lounge on the tree-shaded bottom deck of this hymn to modern architecture, occasionally responding to the Stevensons' texts with "OK," or "See you when you get here." The only little problem was that during that week in Port Aransas I'd already read everything I had on my phone. Not much of a problem, really; my tote bag still held that notebook of Koshan Idrisov's that I'd taken to the beach with me after I threw the rest of his possessions into a couple of cardboard boxes.

It had been nothing more than a slight incongruity that caught my eye, the fact of notes written in a tight, spiky German handwriting among the possessions of a young man from Central Asia. German wasn't a popular language in the 'stans. If the handwriting had been Cyrillic or Arabic, I'd probably have tossed this tightly bound, stained notebook in with the rest of Koshan's junk.

But *German?* And in a script that hardly anybody could read these days? A couple of my professors at the university might have been familiar with it, the old guys who'd done research in Germany back before computers replaced card catalogs. Apart from them, I didn't think anybody in Texas read German script – except me and the other survivors of Frau Heilemann's high school German classes.

I grinned, remembering the glorious revelation those classes had been to me. I'd signed up for French and Spanish in ninth grade only to discover that both classes moved at a pace so glacial, I memorized the dialogues in the textbooks while my classmates were still stumbling over the opening sentences. Tenth grade opened up new worlds with a fanfare of trumpets… or, to put it more prosaically: Frau Heilemann's announcement that God had sent her to Texas for a reason and that His reason was to convey the benefits of German civilization to the young barbarians of Beeville, Texas.

Frau Heilemann employed the time-honored German tradition of *Blitzkrieg*. Students ambled into her classroom expecting to be granted a generous time to warm up their brains after leaving them turned off all summer, and exited in a state of shock clutching handouts on *Fraktur* (a printing style used in Germany until the mid-twentieth century), *Sütterlin* (the traditional spiky handwriting, hereafter to be referred to as 'German script'), *Faust (Part I)* and *Sprich Deutsch: A Conversation Manual*, all of which we were expected to master well before mid-terms. As in, Frau Heilemann suggested, how about next week?

Honors students, meaning kids who cared about their GPA, fell over each other to get out of a class where the teacher hadn't been trained by American educational philosophy to pass out A's to everybody with nicely combed hair. I stayed, loved the atmosphere, learned to love the language, in fact loved everything about the class except Frau Heilemann herself – even for me, that was a German too far. That was okay. I hadn't signed up out of admiration for her sparkling personality, and I didn't stay for that.

I stayed because, for the first time since my incarceration in Beeville, I was *learning* something.

I even learned to scrape my unruly hair back from my face and contain it with elastic bands, rather than listen to Frau Heilemann's comments on people who didn't bother to comb their hair before class. I actually did comb it, it was just that it reverted with reprehensible enthusiasm to its nature as a mass of frizzy curls.

And it wasn't *red*. Bright brown, maybe. Farther than that I would not concede.

Fairness compels me to add that I wasn't any brighter than the honors students diving over the side of that particular ship. My failure to get much out of other subjects might have had something to do with my slacker-style attitude to life and the fact that most Beeville High teachers were too worn down to do more than go through the motions. It was just that something in my brain seized on the patterns of language with delight. I soaked up vocabulary by just reading the lists, and by the second week I could fake my way through an improvised conversation by relying less on consciously memorized grammar than on a feeling that the sentences *wanted* to sound a certain way.

Like I said – my one talent.

Now, with a smile curving my lips at the memory of how thin-lipped, grey-haired little Frau Heilemann had turned my life around and sent me heading for college, I took up Koshan Idrisov's mysterious notebook and gave it the attention I'd omitted to give during that gloriously lazy week at the beach.

The first surprise was that despite the script, it wasn't written in German. Half of it wasn't, anyway. It seemed to be an unordered collection of words and phrases in some language that was totally unfamiliar to me, with German translations and queries jotted down beside them. This language apparently had some sounds that the writer felt traditional script was unable to express, because the transcribed words were peppered with phonetic symbols and explanatory notes in brackets.

After working my way through a couple of pages I put the notebook down and stared over the lake. What language *was* this, anyway, with its jangling sounds and grating syllables, its superfluity of consonants and shortage of vowels?

Thalia Lensky had been in Taklanistan last fall, so it stood to reason that the guide she'd met and subsequently recommended to me was a Taklan. In which case he was probably a speaker of some dialect of Farsi, which was an Indo-European language even if it did look kind of strange to most Europeans.

This language was definitely not Indo-European.

Nor was it Pashto, Uyghur, Kazakh, or any of the other languages common in Central Asia. I didn't actually know those languages, but I could recognize them.

And it was barely even pronounceable.

"Q!z – girl," I muttered. The string of phonetic symbols identified with "!" suggested something like a glottal stop followed by a hacking cough.

"Vlaad – becomes, is becoming." Okay, at least that sounded like a real word.

"Bakhsh# - contented." The hash mark meant… huh, he'd written it out, evidently despairing of phonetic symbolism. "Rocks clashing." How the hell were you supposed to use soft human organs to make a sound like rocks clashing? I gave it the old college try anyway, and felt idiotically pleased with my results. Heck, there was enough here for a complete sentence! I tried it out: "Q!x vlaad bakhsh#."

A cloud must have passed over the sun just then; for a moment there seemed to be less light than before, and I felt as though gravity was swooping around wildly and pulling my bones in different directions. But despite that moment of disorientation, my stab at pronouncing the mystery language didn't sound so bad – and apart from a sudden shooting pain above my right eyebrow, I didn't feel so bad either. In fact, I felt quite gloriously contented with my lot on this earth, right down to my place on this shady deck overlooking the lake. I looked up into a deep blue cloudless sky, feeling as though I could float right up into it – if the sound of an arriving car hadn't distracted me. Here, just to make my cup overflow, were the Stevensons at last. I dry-crunched some aspirin and headed down the curving stone steps from the deck to meet them at their car.

I began to feel somewhat less contented as I walked them through the house. Part of the problem was that small but persistent headache, which made it hard to concentrate on exactly where we were. I'm pretty sure we cycled through one suite of rooms and halls and outer decks two and a half times before I caught on and concentrated on going up the spiral staircase to the next level.

A larger problem, though, was that my loyal ex-student was looking less and less happy. Angie squealed (piercingly) with delight at each wacky architectural feature, and exclaimed at intervals that *nobody* they knew had *anything* like this house (doubtless true: I don't think anybody else had given the architect-developer any money to play with after they saw this place). She even, engagingly, found parallels with Frank Lloyd Wright's architecture in the strangest bits of the house.

Trouble was, Bruce was the one with the family money. And the ambition. He'd achieved tenure in record time, and now he wanted a house that would position him as the obvious successor to the current chairman of the mining engineering department. As we made our way from porthole windows to spiral stairs to cantilevered decks I could practically see him thinking that a listed historical building in West Austin would fit his desired image better than this display of modern architecture running amok.

Which it probably would, but I didn't have a listed historical mansion to show him. What I had was this house, and a growing hunger for the commission on this sale and its effect on my bank account.

I can't think why I even tried it. I blame the headache, which aspirin had barely blunted, and the extreme effort of concentration required to keep in mind where we were in the sprawling house. I just didn't have any mental energy left to tamp down my wild fantasies about how to make Bruce happy with the Harris house.

When he pulled Angie out onto a deck with a murmured apology, I didn't have to eavesdrop to guess at the substance of the conversation. This was the place where Sensible Hubby reads the riot act to Exhilarated Wife, and I could almost hear that nice, fat commission taking wings and fluttering off to land in somebody else's wallet. I would probably never again have clients who could afford a place like this.

That was when I pulled the notebook out of my tote bag, flipped it open and skimmed down the page I'd been reading.

Bummer – there were no words meaning "disgustingly rich clients" that I could shoehorn into that little sentence.

Oh, well, what difference did it make? I was trying to use magic, and since there's no such thing as magic, I could make up my own rules. There was a word for "and".

"Bruce dva Angie vlaad bakhsh#."

The room darkened as though the lights were failing. I had the momentary illusion of being on a roller coaster or inside a gyroscope, with gravity pulling at me from crazy angles. The little needle of pain over my right eyebrow turned into a huge lance aimed right at the back of my eyeball. I groaned involuntarily and bent over for a moment, cupping a hand over my eye.

"Sienna, are you all right?" They were back inside already.

Eins, zwei, drei…"Never better," I lied, forcing a smile. The headache had obviously settled in to torture me for the rest of the day, and now I was going to have to act happy with their decision to do something sensible instead of buying Whitney Harris's white elephant. The girl was definitely no longer contented.

They were smiling too. Both of them.

"Bruce had his doubts, but I've convinced him that this is too good an opportunity to miss," Angie announced buoyantly.

"Yes, well, I certainly understand…" I actually started the little speech I'd been working on, in which I pretended to be a good sport who didn't want them to buy anything they might be unhappy with, before it dawned on me that Angie wasn't saying what I'd been braced for. "I'm sorry, what?" Maybe the pain of this sudden migraine attack was making me hallucinate.

"We'd like you to convey our offer to the seller," Bruce said.

He and Angie looked completely, gloriously contented with their decision. I wasn't.

The girl was scared stiff.

6. Taking the relationship to a different level

Edward Osborne stared at the IT report in disgust. After he'd been unable to find any Alt-Shaimaki materials on Idrisov's laptop except for three scans of notebook pages – one of them slightly blurred but still barely legible – he had handed the thing over to a computer science expert for detailed examination. A risky step, but he had some protection; Jackson's wife was one of his dissertation candidates. Nobody who'd written eighty percent of a reasonably good dissertation would risk upsetting their major professor this close to the finish line, and he made it clear to Carrie Jackson's husband that any careless gossiping about this little job would seriously upset him.

And surely it was a risk worth taking. The data *had* to be there, somewhere, concealed in one of those sneaky ways that only computer people knew about.

Except, according to Carrie's husband, it wasn't.

He reported that the laptop was quite new, a Chinese knockoff of a Dell model, and that the previous owner had not been a particularly sophisticated user. He'd found a handful of emails to and from just one other person, a browser history heavy on gambling sites and soft porn, and three scanned images. That was it.

"Could data have been loaded onto a flash drive and then erased from the computer?"

Jackson shrugged. "*Could* be… but I didn't find any evidence of erased files. And I don't believe in a user sophisticated enough to move data without leaving tracks, but too stupid to clear the cookies left by porn sites. Dr. Osborne, this computer is the equivalent of the used car owned by a little old lady who only used it to drive to church on Sundays. Except," he added thoughtfully, "considering the browsing history, the owner was no lady. Where did you say you got this again?"

"Just doing a favor for a friend," Osborne said vaguely. He got rid of Jackson and snarled quietly at the worthless laptop. Idrisov must have had a lot of Alt-Shaimaki data to sell, if he was willing to float scans of whole pages of vocabulary and phrases to attract a buyer. The rest of that data had to be *somewhere*: if not here, then among Idrisov's belongings – wherever they were.

The emails gave him a clue to that, at least. Exchanges between Idrisov and some woman vaguely connected with the math department, they accounted for Idrisov's invitation to speak at the conference and strengthened Osborne's conviction that there was valuable data concealed just beyond his reach. Idrisov had originally contacted this woman in search of buyers for this information. That in itself didn't say where he'd hidden it, but the last emails in the exchange pointed him to a place to look. This Thalia Lensky had done one last favor for her Taklanistani buddy, finding a place for him to stay in some house near campus whose owner had a room for rent.

Osborne couldn't think of a student whose arm he could twist for the next job, so he actually hired a P.I. to gain access to Koshan Idrisov's room and go through his belongings.

The man was a bungler.

First the P.I. had let the landlady see him, pretending to be interested in renting that particular room. She told him it was already rented, and of course he couldn't very well tell her that her tenant was probably dead; for that matter, Osborne had been too cautious to give the P.I. that piece of information. When he reported failure, Osborne told him to break into the room and ransack it.

"You're not paying me enough to take that kind of chance."

"If you don't produce what I need," Osborne said, "I'm not paying you anything at all."

After the bumbling idiot reported a second failure – evidently he had spooked the old lady, who ran him off at gunpoint – Osborne did, in fact, wind up paying the man just to ensure his silence.

And he still hadn't set eyes on Idrisov's store of Alt-Shaimaki vocabulary and phrases!

He was beginning to think that he might have to take a hand personally. What had happened to Koshan Idrisov just might also have to happen to the old lady who'd rented him a room, if she persisted in blocking his access to data which he now considered morally his. After all, he probably would have paid Idrisov for the information. If the man had lived. It wasn't his fault that everything had gone wrong.

As for the P.I.'s story about being threatened with a gun – he wasn't too worried about that. Some old broad with palsied hands, waving a gun she was probably too stupid to have loaded properly? Not a problem for a man who had the secret of disappearance on the tip of his tongue.

I badly wanted to talk over the day's happenings with Laura, my best friend and also my long-term tenant since the middle of our sophomore year. But when I got home, she wasn't there.

Worse: Craig was.

He was sitting in the living room that Laura and I shared, drinking beer and watching TV, with his feet up on the coffee table. Cath Palug was nowhere to be seen, but that wasn't surprising; he regularly exercised his secret superpower of invisibility when we entertained people he considered unworthy of his attentions, and Craig had never been a favorite of his.

Laura and I were modestly proud of the way we'd redecorated the living room. My parents, who never noticed their surroundings as long as there was enough light to read academic journals by, had allowed it to age ungracefully into a dim brown space filled with large brown furniture. When Laura moved in with me, we sold the heavy old-fashioned furniture and painted the room light gray. Our redecorating was limited by my insistence on paying half the cost and by the fact that all I had to spend was what I could get for the old furniture, so it wasn't as spiffy as Laura's two rooms-and-bathroom suite, but we were happy with it. An Ikea coffee table paired with a blue-gray striped futon couch and chairs made the place look light and airy. The finishing touch was the replacement of my grandparents' monster cabinet TV with a wall-mounted flat screen.

I didn't feel that Craig's invasion really improved the look of the room. His blond curls and carefully nurtured three-day blond stubble no longer appealed to me. Had they ever, really?

"Hey, babe!" he greeted me. "Come over and take a load off. Let your hair down – well, let it escape anyway, ha ha!" A wide-spread arm invited me to sit on his lap. I took a chair on the other side of the coffee table.

Craig looked hurt. "Why so unfriendly? Here I am to solve all your problems, don't I even get a little kiss? And babe, somebody's dumped a bunch of junk in my room. You need to clean it out."

I learned that Laura had let him in before going off for a late-afternoon rehearsal with one of the bands she sang for. A communications problem. She didn't know that my feelings towards Craig had changed; to be fair, I hadn't been aware of how much they'd changed until I walked into my house to find him making himself so very much at home.

And, of course, Laura also didn't know that Michael Ryan had rented the room that Koshan had vacated without warning.

So when Craig showed up, announcing that he was going to solve all my financial problems by renting the vacant room himself and that I agreed it was high time we took our relationship to the next level, Laura had no particular reason to disbelieve him. She probably thought a little less of me, but that would have made her even less willing to question him.

I told him the first reason why I wasn't going to clear the room out for him, the one that had nothing to do with our relationship.

The shock of my news made him actually drop his feet to the floor and sit up. "What do you mean, somebody else has the room? We agreed I was going to take it over!"

"No. *We* did not agree on anything. You told me that was how it was going to be, and I went down to the beach to think it over."

"Well, you didn't tell me no!"

Aunt Georgia always said, "Count to three before you shoot your mouth off, Sienna." *Um, dois, três…* "I'm doing that now."

"You can't change your mind on me like that!"

This argument had creepy echoes of an older and nastier one. I took a

41

breath and reminded myself that this was *Craig*, not a drunken stranger. But it didn't help. *Acel, aryo, adek.* I've never learned Acholi, but it's interesting, isn't it, that all the numerals start with 'a'? Thinking about that made me feel stronger. "I'm not changing my mind, Craig. I never said yes in the first place."

"If you didn't say no, that's the same thing as agreeing!"

I shook my head and he switched arguments, perhaps sensing that this one was a loser. "So where did you meet this Mike Ryan? Down at the beach? He must be real hot stuff, huh, if you're dumping me for him."

"Craig, I'm not dumping you for him."

"Sure feels like it."

"No." I thought over exactly what I wanted to say and counted to five this time. In Japanese. *Ichi, ni, san, yon, go.* "I'm dumping you for *me*."

"Huh?"

"Think of it," I advised him, "as moving our relationship to a different level."

That week away from Craig's expectations and assumptions had been extremely clarifying. Even Floss and Blossom had been helpful. "When you talk about this guy," Floss had said, "you don't sound as if you have fun with him."

"That's not the only thing in life."

"No, but it's important," Blossom said. "What do you actually get out of hanging out with this guy?"

I shrugged. "He's good-looking enough, and he seemed to be really into me for some reason. I thought maybe, if we got to know each other, it would get better. With time. I'm no good at judging character, Bloss. So I've been trying not to judge."

Both girls rolled their eyes.

"Well, I can hardly just dump him when he hasn't done anything wrong!"

"Sure you can," said Floss.

"It'd be a kindness," Blossom said.

"Why let him waste any more time with you, when you really don't even like him much?"

It had sounded more reasonable in Port Aransas than it did in my living room.

Craig spent some time telling me how unreasonable I was being, how *unfair*, how I didn't appreciate all he'd done for me. Apparently he valued his company very highly, if a dozen evenings listening to Laura singing with various bands constituted a gift for which I owed him lifelong gratitude. When he got to the point of whining about how I'd taken him for granted and he'd wasted all this time and money on a girl who didn't even put out, I reminded him that my housemate had given us free passes to all those shows.

That made him so incandescently angry that I wondered if I should head for the bedroom, but he ran out of things to say and stormed out before I was quite ready to introduce him to my father's old Smith and Wesson.

And now I had *two* concerns to talk over with Laura when she drifted into the house after rehearsal.

Laura's side of the house mirrored mine, structurally: two bedrooms with a bathroom between that opened into both rooms. The floor plan had allowed the architect to save on hall space in the interests of putting a generous living room and kitchen between the two pairs of bedrooms, but it made it awkward if you were trying to rent out rooms. Laura had both bedrooms and the bathroom on her side, and paid well for the privilege, but it meant that when I was cash-strapped the only remaining space to rent out was the bedroom that shared a bathroom with my room. For several years I'd rented that to an elderly retired Italian teacher who did little but sit in her room reading, but earlier this year Mrs. Costellano's daughter had finally produced the grandson she'd all but given up hoping for. Suddenly the woman just had to move to Denver to live with her daughter and grandson, and a chunk of my monthly income went with her.

All of which was why I'd never gotten around to decorating my side of the house as Laura had done with hers, and why her spare room was a much pleasanter place to sit and grouch about life than my bedroom was. Laura was an Anglophile with a serious addiction to Liberty floral cotton prints. Sometimes I thought she overdid it, but what the heck – unlike me, she had plenty of money to spend doing up the place, and on a hot summer afternoon like this it was very pleasant to sit in a room that looked like an English flower garden run amok. With a river at the bottom of the garden – that was represented by the watery blue-green curtains behind the floral-print throw pillows.

Being an Austin slacker is a lot easier if you have a trust fund behind you, rather than only an aging house that eats its head off in running repairs. Not that I should complain; I haven't had to get a real job yet.

But I did, quietly, envy Laura her financial resources. And maybe a few other things, like her talent – she didn't get gigs singing for three bands just because of her pretty black eyes and crisply curling black hair – and, oh, her self-assurance, her social skills, her empathy…

All of which were now focused on me and my confused kvetching about the day.

"I had no idea you felt that way about Craig," she said for the fourth or fifth time, "or I'd never have let him in. I'm so sorry—"

"Oh, stop apologizing! I'm not sure *I* knew I felt that way about Craig, until he tried to bully me into letting him move in here."

"I thought you guys were getting along okay before you went off to stay with Floss and Blossom."

"I thought so too, but they persuaded me my standards ought to be higher. They felt that 'I don't actually mind hanging out with him, as long as it's not too often,' wasn't good enough."

"Well, I've been trying to tell you that for years!" Laura said, her black eyes sparkling with indignation. "It's about time you heard it from *somebody* – even the Candyfloss Twins."

I shook my head. "You know how it is, Laura. I'm just not a good judge of character."

"I know no such thing," Laura said promptly. "What I know is, you made one dumb mistake when we were sophomores and you have never trusted your own judgment again. And," she added, "at least half of that mistake, if not more, was your aunt's fault. What did she think she was doing, giving an eighteen-year-old girl the keys to a whole house west of campus?"

"Making it possible for me to go to the university?"

Laura snorted. "She could have let you move in with her."

"Aunt Georgia values her privacy."

"All the same, it was irresponsible of her!"

My parents had died in an airplane accident, returning from a conference, the summer I was twelve. I'd been lucky that I had family who swooped in to take care of me. My mother's sister Milly in Beeville had taken me in with her own slightly younger children; I may have done a lot of baby-sitting, and I never learned to love Beeville, but I knew I was lucky to be with my own family instead of being thrown to the mercy of social services. And Aunt Georgia had rented out my parents' house to help Aunt Milly and Uncle Max with the extra expense of raising me.

When I graduated from Beeville High at eighteen, to my own astonishment the recipient of the Augusta Engelberger Germanic Studies scholarship to the University of Texas, Aunt Georgia had decided that the house would be better used as a place for me to live than as a source of income. I could always pick up tutoring jobs on campus for a bit of extra cash. So I had become the proud possessor of a set of house keys, the family photo albums, and my father's Smith and Wesson. Which last I did not learn to use until after the unpleasant incident Laura was referring to. I had no wish to revisit that episode now.

"Whatever," I said. "It was a long time ago, and it really doesn't bother me any more."

"Liar," Laura said without heat. "Want some ice cream? I picked up some Belgian Toffee Chocolate Chip from Amy's on the way home."

Best offer I'd had all day, even counting the Stevensons' offer for the Harris mansion.

Over the ice cream she started trying again to apologize about letting Craig in, and I told her again to shut up. "You didn't know he was lying. And you couldn't have known about the new tenant, because I went off to the office before you were up this morning." Trying to find a way to ditch the new tenant, actually.

"Oh, right, you said you showed a listing this afternoon! How did that go?"

I rubbed my right eye, where the memory of that sudden migraine still lingered. "All right, I guess. That's really what I wanted to talk to you about. It, uh, kind of freaked me out."

"Did they make an offer or didn't they?"

"Oh, they did. They actually offered the asking price!" I mentioned the awe-inspiring sum that Bruce Stevenson hadn't even blinked at. "There's no way it won't be accepted."

Laura got the slightly misty-eyed expression that meant she was doing math in her head. I'd known three separate guys who thought she returned their devotion when she looked like that, only to discover that the expression vanished when she finished her calculus homework. "Why aren't you happier? Shouldn't the commission on that set you up financially for a while? You won't need the rent from that room. If you really want your privacy, you won't even need *my* rent," she said, her voice wobbling slightly.

I got up and circled around the bowls of melting ice cream to hug her. "Don't be silly. You're not just a tenant, you're my friend and my sanity. What would I do without you, Laura Jacobson?"

"Probably make a lot more stupid mistakes," Laura said, with a suppressed sniffle. "All right, then, what's worrying you about the Stevenson commission?"

I tried to tell her about the strange things that had happened around that showing, and she tried to look as though she was paying serious attention. But her lips kept twitching.

"So tell me," I finished, "what the hell you find so *funny* about this situation!"

A giggle escaped. "All of it? Oh, except for your migraine; I'm sorry about that. Is it better now?"

I rubbed my forehead. "It went away a while ago. I guess about the time when I was throwing Craig out."

"Now that," Laura said, "could be deeply meaningful. But the rest of the story? Come on, Sienna. A mystery language that has been seen only in a notebook belonging to your disappearing tenant? And you took one look at the notes and decided that the language could be used to do *magic*? What have you been smoking lately?"

I held up my spoon. "Ice cream is my drug of choice. And I didn't even have that when I was out by the lake today."

"Well, then. There's no such thing as magic, Sienna. You probably turned on your extra-charming mode with Bruce Stevenson when he started to look unhappy –"

"I don't do that!"

"Oh, yes you do. I've seen you in action before. And don't get mad. Where's the harm in it? You'll get a nice commission, Angie Stevenson gets the showpiece of a house that'll turn her into a social leader, and Bruce… can't buy the chairmanship anyway, so he might as well spend his money on a mansion. What's the problem?"

I couldn't think of one, when she put it like that. I scraped the last bits of toffee chunks and chocolate chips out of my bowl. "I think I need more ice cream."

7. Secret energy

Most of the next day was wasted on a Realtors' Continuing Education class that Aunt Georgia chased me to. Oh, she was right to do so; Texas expects realtors to waste a certain number of hours every two years on this nonsense if we want to renew our licenses, and Aunt Georgia had been generous enough to pay my fees for the bargain package course she'd signed us up for this year.

It's just that there's "Continuing Education," and then there's "Continuous Nonsense," and by me, this particular section of the package course was definitely in the latter category. It consisted of one very long presentation by a wild-eyed, wild-haired lady who had, in my opinion, been fatally influenced by Prosperity Gospel and other heresies. Normally I can sit through these required classes without too much strain. After all, it's six to eight hours during which I can't be expected to do anything else, and a girl can always use some quiet time to rethink her current nail polish and lipstick color scheme. During "Breaking Barriers: Fair Housing," I had decided to switch from Pink Magnolia to Coral Cay, and that had turned out very well.

But after the first half hour of "The Gospel of GREAT (Great Real EstATe)," I was in danger of breaking my pretty pink coral fingernails. It was that hard to hold myself back from jumping up and screaming at the speaker. In self-defense, I scribbled twice as hard on the legal pad in my brown leather folder. She glanced at me approvingly; there probably weren't many people in her captive audience who seemed so dedicated to capturing her pearls of wisdom.

She wouldn't have been quite so approving if she'd been able to read what

I was writing. It started with, "No! Jesus does NOT want you to be rich! He doesn't care about that!" and went on through, "Dear God, can you possibly be so clueless that when Jesus said, 'In my Father's house are many mansions,' you thought He meant, 'I have some really great listings?'"

German script came in handy today, because I didn't want anybody reading over my shoulder and getting mad about my reactions. If I'd learned nothing else from Frau Heilemann, I would still have been eternally grateful to her for teaching me that one thing. It made it possible to cover most of a page with my complaints while appearing to be a serious student taking this witch seriously. Even when she strolled down between our desks to sneak a peek at my notes, she had no clue what I'd been writing.

I was really, really tempted to bail at the lunch break, the more so when my phone (which liked me again, now that it could see my hair) told me there was a message on my voicemail from Dr. Edward Osborne. He remembered me? Amazing. I'd been one of a hundred insignificant freshmen in the survey course on historical linguistics where he only gave one lecture out of five, leaving the heavy lifting to his T.A.

I decided to put off listening to the message until we got sprung for the day. That way I could while away the second half of this ghastly lecture by speculating on just what bit of linguistic brilliance I'd displayed in that class to make Dr. Osborne remember me from nine years ago.

When the class was over and I checked my voicemail, my castles in the air melted like ice cream in August. He didn't remember me as a student of his at all: the message was for Koshan Idrisov's landlady. My tenant, Dr. Osborne said, had brought up some interesting points about Central Asian languages when they met at the conference. He wished to meet with me and discuss Koshan's work farther. He suggested we meet at Quack's that evening; would eight o'clock be too late?

Clearly my name had meant less than nothing to him. There went my self-image: from brilliantly memorable linguistics student to anonymous landlady in four short hours. *Sic transit gloria mundi.* Or as we say in the vernacular, that's the way the cookie crumbles.

I fired off a quick text saying that I'd be there and headed back to enjoy the peace of my own house for a nice break before the meeting. Not that it worked out quite like that.

This time the intruder in my living room was somebody who had a legitimate key to the house, more's the pity.

Michael Ryan.

He was lounging on the futon couch much as Craig had done yesterday, only he managed somehow to look neat and compact rather than a sprawling mess. He got to his feet when I came in, and I noticed with begrudging approval that he'd placed his loafers by the door before putting his feet up on the furniture. Big deal. Just because he wasn't as obnoxious as some people didn't mean I had to like having his company forced on me.

"Sit, sit," I said, waving my styrofoam box from Milto's in his direction. "I'm just passing through." I could eat in the kitchen.

"Is that dinner?"

"Great deduction, Sherlock." I was feeling virtuous; instead of giving in to the lust for gyros with tzatziki that Milto's often inspires in me, I'd settled for the large Greek salad.

He sniffed the air. "Salad for dinner? Do you really find that satisfying?"

Well, no, but after dining on Belgian Toffee Chocolate Chip ice cream the previous night it had seemed like a sensible course correction.

"I've just ordered a pizza," he said now. "I'd be willing to share."

I paused on my way through the room.

"Italian sausage, sweet red peppers, and double mushrooms," he said, sounding like somebody leaning out of a car to offer candy to a kid. "And *Gaslight* is about to start."

Charles Boyer, Ingrid Bergman *and* double mushrooms? Worked for me. I set the salad box down on the coffee table. "I have to be somewhere at eight," I said.

"It's the early movie, it'll be over in time."

By the time I'd brought plates and forks from the kitchen, the pizza was here and the credits were rolling and I was all ready to immerse myself in Ingrid Bergman's tribulations. Cath Palug, demonstrating his poor taste in companions, was rolling around in front of the coffee table and inviting Michael to tickle his tummy.

"Don't fall for the cat's blandishments," I warned him. "We keep a fully stocked first aid kit for people who think he wants them to pet him."

"Do you?" Michael reached down between the couch and the coffee table and ruffled the white fur on Cath Palug's stomach. With impunity.

"Quisling," I told the cat.

"Is that his name?"

"No, it's a description of his morals. Or lack thereof. We've been calling him Cath Palug."

"CaspalAG? What kind of name is that?" He put the stress on the last syllable.

"Cath PALug," I said, moving the stress back where it belonged. "Welsh. He was one of the three great plagues of the island of Ynys Môn. And this guy is the great plague of the house of Sienna Brown."

"You speak Welsh?"

"No, I read about him when I was studying Middle French. There's one poem in which Cath Palug – or Chapalu in the French version – is said to have drowned King Arthur in a bog and taken his place on the throne. After the third or fourth time this guy almost shoved me out of bed, I decided that he was clearly a reincarnation of the Welsh monster-cat."

"Strange tastes," Michael said softly. "*I* wouldn't do that."

What, shove me out of bed? "Not going to be an issue."

He ignored that.

"Would your other tenant like to join us?"

Laura's side of the house was dark. "I expect she's out. Singing somewhere," I expanded.

"What, this early?"

"Probably letting somebody buy her dinner before the first show. She's out most evenings." I was a little surprised at myself for saying so much; usually I'm a bit cagier when it comes to admitting that I'm often alone in the house at night. But for all he'd inadvertently terrified me on our first meeting, Michael Ryan was coming across now as so completely unthreatening that I couldn't keep feeling nervous of him. Maybe it wouldn't be so bad having him as a tenant after all.

The pizza toppings, as well as those he'd listed, also included black olives and pepperoni and caramelized onions. Yep. Potentially an excellent tenant, I thought, digging in.

For the first hour or so we munched and watched companionably, just enjoying Boyer and Bergman. He commented favorably on the chunks of white feta and the big, salty black olives in the Greek salad; I complimented him on his choice of pizza toppings. He went back to the kitchen and got a couple of cold beers out of the refrigerator; I accepted one.

"I never can understand," he commented after a while, "why Bergman doesn't see how Boyer is manipulating her."

"Once people make you doubt your own perceptions, they have incredible power over you."

"Yes, but why doesn't she trust her own perceptions? That's the bit I don't get."

"You've never been in a situation like that."

"Oh, and I suppose you have?"

I shouldn't have accepted that beer. *Yek, do, se.* This conversation was reminding me painfully of why I'd studied Farsi. "Some of us don't need to live through a thing in order to understand it," I evaded. I wished he would shut up. "Can we just watch the movie already?"

Not when Michael Ryan had his teeth in an argument, we couldn't. This was my first experience of one of his major character flaws: he couldn't just let things go.

"Sure," he said, and immediately afterwards: "Suppose I told you that this was a vegetarian pizza. Would that be enough to make you think you'd imagined the Italian sausage topping?"

"It doesn't work like that."

"It seems to in this movie."

"No." I could practically feel my hair writhing against the double scrunchie that was supposed to hold it down. The more annoyed I got, the more it seemed to express its inner frizziness. How could he be so dense? "Boyer doesn't start with crude, obvious lies that can be easily disproved. He nibbles away at her memories, her feelings… It would be more like gaslighting if you told me… oh… that I came home while you were in the living room because I secretly wanted to spend time with you, even if I hadn't admitted it to myself."

"*Do* you secretly want to spend time with me?" He looked hopeful.

"Not if you're going to continue spoiling a perfectly good movie by arguing."

"I *can* be quiet. With an incentive like that."

Incentive? I blinked and mentally replayed the last few things I'd said. "Oh. That was a purely hypothetical argument."

He leaned toward me, extending a hand. "Any chance of translating it out of the theoretical realm?"

How had we ended up sitting side by side on the couch? This man was suddenly *way* too close. "None!" I set my beer down. I could feel the heat from his body – it was like an assault, having him so near me that I could feel how tense he was – what the hell happened to casually bickering over an old movie? Somehow he was making everything I said mean – far more than I'd intended. And he was looking at me as though he really cared about my response.

"I have to go." I couldn't get up fast enough.

"Huh? What did I do now?"

"Nothing," I said, pushing my feet back into my sandals, "I told you I had to be somewhere later."

"You've got time to finish the movie."

"I've lost interest."

"Wait! When will you be back?"

"Later." I found my keys in the tote bag. "Don't wait up."

I was way early for the meeting with Dr. Osborne. Fortunately, Quack's wasn't crowded. I got some hibiscus lemonade and a peach cobbler muffin to make up for the pizza and salad I'd abandoned, and settled down in a back corner. I needed a little calming-down time anyway; I wasn't quite sure why I'd reacted so strongly to what had to be the mildest hint of a pass I'd ever cut off. Replaying the conversation, I wasn't even sure Michael Ryan had been making a pass. There was just something irritating about that man, something that made me over-react to every little thing. I really didn't greet most new acquaintances with a loaded gun, or walk out on them over a disagreement about an old movie. I wasn't that difficult to deal with... was I?

Laura would have reassured me, but she wasn't available. I pulled out Koshan's mystery notebook again; thinking about languages always refreshed my spirit.

Because of the plethora of special symbols, reading the notebook was slow going. It was even slower because I normally take in languages through speech and hearing, rather than just reading written or printed words. And after yesterday's showing of the Harris place, I was making a conscious effort *not* to subvocalize as I puzzled my way through the tortured script.

Not that it could really make any difference, of course. I was not insane. I didn't believe that spoken words could give me a headache, much less persuade a reluctant client to make an offer on a property. It just seemed prudent not to take any chances, that was all.

I worked my way through another page and a half of seriously vowel-deprived words and phrases, acquiring more vocabulary than I ever expected to need for describing the condition of wool or the dryness of yak-dung patties but still coming up blank on clues to this language's place in the great family of human speech.

Linguists don't *like* languages that turn up without relatives. We like to slot even the most remote examples into some kind of family tree. Joseph Greenberg shoved the !Kung language of Botswana into a shakily defined "family" of other African languages on the flimsy basis that they all used click consonants; earlier linguists had invented the category of Finno-Ugric languages just to keep Finnish and Hungarian from getting lonely.

And my mind was running over these examples because, like the language documented in Koshan's notebook, they generally had an excess of consonants and a shortage of vowels and sounded as if someone were spraying the room with a machine gun full of k's and d's and worse. Just look at this word that was annotated, "secret energy," in German. "*Ysh!mqvad.*" I couldn't stop myself from trying to say it—

Nothing happened.

Absolutely nothing.

Except that a few crumbs of peach muffin fell into the notebook, and it didn't take magic to account for that. I closed the notebook and slipped it into my tote bag, and flipped open my brown leather folder to doodle on the legal pad while I waited. It would be very bad form to hand over a notebook marred with grease spots and tea stains to Dr. Osborne.

I doodled a little rectangle on the page of my "notes" from the Gospel Seminar.

I *was* going to give it to him, wasn't I?

I added lines below and to the right of the rectangle, making it look like the top of a stack of pages.

Dr. Osborne didn't exactly have the warmest personality among the linguistics faculty, but that didn't matter. The important thing was that he was a real scholar, someone who would be able to place this language, someone who could use the information contained in the notebook to add another tiny scrap to the vast edifice of human knowledge. A far more suitable recipient of Koshan Idrisov's work than Koshan's scatty landlady who didn't even have a real job, who was delusional enough to think that some of the words in the notebook had actually given her a headache and… I suppressed the memory of Bruce and Angie Stevenson's surprise offer on the Harris house. That had nothing to do with language.

Nothing at all.

As Laura had reminded me, there was no such thing as magic.

I scrawled, "*Ysh!mqvad*" below the doodle of a stack of pages. In German script, as spiky looking as the word sounded. Said it again under my breath. See? Nothing happened.

Of course, it had been just one word, not a *sentence*.

At last I saw Dr. Osborne's square glasses and pointy little goatee at the bakery counter. Finally, someone who could take this notebook and the uncomfortable mysteries surrounding it off my hands! I waved but he didn't seem to see me.

I would be happy to put this material in the hands of somebody who knew what to do with it. Wouldn't I?

"Dr. Osborne! Over here!"

He was still staring into the bakery case. I grabbed my tote bag – no way was I going to leave my wallet and keys unattended in a busy coffee shop – and opened out my leather folder on the table top to signify that this place was taken. I stepped between a pair of giant rucksacks belonging to some guys with very big feet and tapped my ex-professor on the shoulder. "I've got a table in the corner."

He gave me a blank stare. "I'm sorry, do I know you?"

"You asked me to meet you here. Koshan Idrisov rented a room from me," I explained, suppressing all mention of historical linguistics survey classes. If he'd continued nominally giving that class every year, that would be close to a thousand more undergraduates he'd ignored since I took the course. It had been ridiculous to think he'd remember me. "I'm Sienna Brown."

"Oh! I was expecting somebody older." He looked almost embarrassed. Almost human.

"I know," I said, turning up my smile to what Laura called my 'extra-charming mode.' "It's that word 'landlady,' isn't it? The connotations are *so* misleading."

"Indeed," said Dr. Osborne drily.

I led the way back to the corner table I'd claimed, slung my tote bag into the corner and took the chair beside it.

"Idrisov claimed to have knowledge of a hitherto unknown language spoken in a valley of the High Pamirs," Osborne said while pulling his chair out, "but he disappeared from the conference before I could look over the papers he wanted to give me. Did he leave them with you?"

For some reason, the last word I'd scribbled on the legal pad seemed to be blinking at me, the letters swelling and then shrinking again. "*Ysh!mqvad – ysh!mqvad – ysh!mqvad.*"

Secret – secret – secret.

Energy - energy – energy.

Üks, kaks, kolm, I recited mentally. (Estonian is a very strange language.)

Why was Dr. Osborne demanding the papers with his very first words?

"I don't know what happened to Koshan," I said, answering the question

I thought any decent human being should have asked first. "He just — disappeared. It was very strange."

"But he left his effects with you."

Dr. Osborne was hunched over the table now, staring at me through those square-framed glasses. His grad students used to have a running joke about those glasses: you weren't really in trouble, they said, until he took them off.

"There was some junk in the room he'd rented. Nothing valuable. Clothes, a couple of magazines, toiletries. I've packed everything up in case he comes back or sends somebody for his stuff."

"You can give the boxes to me. If anybody inquires, just refer them to me. You don't have to trouble yourself any more."

Just what I'd wanted — wasn't it? To hand over the last trailing bits of Koshan's chaos to somebody else?

Secret energy.

I needed a moment to think. *Wahid, ithnan, thalatha.* Arabic number names aren't nearly as easy to learn as Arabic numerals. "I'd need authorization to do that," I heard myself saying. "From Koshan or a member of his family."

"Don't be stupid! Nobody is going to come looking for secondhand clothes belonging to a Taklanistani visa-jumper!"

He had taken his glasses off, and the blaze of fury in his eyes terrified me. I know scholarly research is more of a cut-throat business than anybody outside the academic world would believe. Even so, this seemed excessive.

It was excessive if Koshan's notes were really nothing more than vocabulary and phrases for yet another little-known Central Asian dialect.

But if they were more than that? If there really was some, oh, all right, some 'secret energy,' bound up in those words?

The man glaring across the table at me was not somebody I wanted to see wielding that energy.

Suddenly all I wanted was to get out of there.

"You can come to the house some time and look through Koshan's belongings," I said, without even waiting to count and think. I stood up and tugged the tote bag strap over my shoulder. "Call me, set up a time."

"Ms. Brown!" Dr. Osborne called after me before I'd even navigated the rucksacks-and-boots hazard.

I looked back.

He was holding my brown leather real estate folder.

"You forgot this."

8. Dead man's shoes

I spent the next morning dealing with the second folder Aunt Georgia had pressed on me. These clients weren't nearly so rewarding as the Stevensons; they were first-time home buyers who wanted to look at everything that was within their price range as well as a lot of homes that were hopelessly beyond their means. Austin itself was definitely out of their range; I drove them to view condos in San Marcos, new homes in Hutto, fixer-uppers in Elgin, scribbling notes in my folder as I went along. The page I'd filled with complaints about that Continuing Ed course seemed to have fallen off the pad, so at least I didn't have to tear it out and crumple it up; but that was about the only luck I encountered.

"We really want our *own* place. These condos are – it would feel just like living in an apartment."

I couldn't argue with that.

"I hear some of these new subdivisions are pretty shoddy work, the homes start falling apart after just a few years," they said in Hutto.

I'd heard the same thing.

"Is your husband handy with tools?" I asked after I put a foot through the front porch of the disaster in Elgin.

"No," he said before his wife could open her mouth. "I do analytics for retail clients who want to optimize their social media presence."

On the drive back to Sweet Georgia Realty he explained exactly what that meant, but I didn't take it in. I was too busy blessing Dr. Edward Osborne, who'd been so pushy when he called that I'd agreed to meet him at the house in early afternoon rather than devoting the entire day to Mr. and Mrs. Newlywed. By now that seemed like a brilliant decision. I could use a break from them, and they could use some time to think over what their bank had told them about possible loans. At present there was an extremely large gap between what they wanted to buy and what they could conceivably get a mortgage for. Part of my job as their real estate representative was to reduce the size of that gap by gently reminding them of reality as we toured possible listings. I'd done my best in that direction, but they were still several learning experiences away from an actual loan.

When I pulled up in front of my own house, I felt like getting out and kissing the threshold. My clients would have thought they'd died and gone to heaven if they'd been able to buy a place like the one I inherited through no virtue of my own. A real house, not a condo with tissue-thin walls or a piece of suburban blight! And in central Austin! Once again I was humbled to recollect how lucky I was. And once again I vowed that I would do whatever it took, including working seriously at the real estate business, to keep paying those astronomical property taxes. I would *not* lose this house. Ever.

Parked just in front of my car was a reminder of what I had to put up with to keep the house: a little red sports car that I had already learned to associate with Michael Ryan. Didn't the man have a job to go to?

The large sedan across the street disgorged Dr. Osborne. Ten minutes early! I suppressed an eye-roll. Good thing I'd prepared to receive him before going off on the real estate tour from hell this morning. I greeted him politely and invited him into my living room. At least it was cool indoors.

"When I decided to rent the room again, I packed up Koshan Idrisov's clothes and shoes in these boxes," I told him, indicating the two medium-sized cardboard boxes I'd asked Michael to put on the coffee table that morning so that Osborne and I wouldn't have to disturb him. "I can't let you just take them away, but you're welcome to look through them to see if you can find your papers."

This was all such a stupid charade. I knew that nothing in those boxes rightfully belonged to Edward Osborne, and he knew it too. But I was willing to pretend I'd fallen for his claim that Koshan had meant to give some papers to him. It was worth it to get him off my back. I figured he'd go through the contents of the boxes with a fine-toothed comb, see that there was nothing in there relating to mysterious Central Asian languages, and go away.

The first part went as I'd anticipated, with the minor exception that Michael Ryan came out of his bedroom and settled on one of the blue and gray striped chairs to watch the macabre exploration of Koshan's effects – these boxes that I was unwillingly beginning to think of as a dead man's possessions. Perhaps, as the Austin police believed, Koshan had disappeared as part of a plan to overstay his visa indefinitely. But he hadn't been rich, or he wouldn't have asked Thalia to find him an inexpensive place to stay for a month, would he? You'd think he would have come back for his clothes.

If he'd been able to.

"You don't have to stick around," I murmured to Michael as Osborne ripped off the tape closing the top box. "I asked you to move the stuff out here so we wouldn't disturb you."

"Somebody needs to look out for your interests," Michael said, equally quietly.

My interests? I didn't care what happened to the stuff in these boxes. I just wasn't – quite – ready to throw it out yet. Felt too much like declaring Koshan Idrisov dead.

My cool, peaceful gray and blue living room seemed to be humming with tension as the two men faced off over the pitiful little remnants of Koshan's trip to America. Oh, nobody *said* anything, but there were whole speeches' worth of body language being exchanged.

Dr. Osborne hunched protectively over the boxes, pulling out one item at a time, shaking, folding, pinching and making sure there was nothing concealed inside the shirt, or the sock, or the underwear that he was holding.

Michael watched him like a hawk, eyes focused on the professor's hands as though he expected him to try and shove one of Koshan's spare shoes into his coat pocket. At the same time he kept an eye on me; every time I stirred, he started to react.

I watched the two of them watching each other and wondered if there was something going on that I didn't know about, or was I merely looking at another instance of testosterone poisoning? Certainly there was enough masculine ego present to account for some tension. Michael's air of barely contained energy, of explosive potential, made him the kind of guy who became the center of any room he walked into without even trying. As for Dr. Osborne, he had been the tenured tyrant of the linguistics department for so long that he'd probably forgotten how to talk to people who weren't afraid of him.

Finally Osborne finished with the last items in the second box – a couple of magazines that he'd gone through page by page as though he thought he'd find a vocabulary and grammar interleaved between *those* kinds of pictures. I was slightly impressed by the fact that he didn't blush. I felt like washing my hands by the time he finished inspecting the magazines, and I hadn't even been touching them. Funny, I'd thought people looked at those kind of pictures on the Internet nowadays. I guess some people always prefer hard-copy.

"There are no papers here," he announced.

"No shit, Sherlock," Michael mocked him.

He ignored that and glared at me. "*What did you do with them?*"

A vital part of a realtor's coping skills, according to Aunt Georgia, is the ability to lie with a straight face. *Un, deux, trois.* I gave him my best blank look, the one I used on bank officers asking me what part of a client's work history had given me the illusion they would qualify for a single dollar in loans. "I don't know what you are talking about. Two weeks ago I packed up everything Koshan left here in those boxes and I haven't looked at them since."

"That won't fly," he snarled, moving towards me. "I *know* you have seen what I'm looking for – I *know* – "

Several things happened at once.

I stepped back. *Not* running away from Dr. Osborne; instinctively heading for the gun safe in my bedroom.

Osborne snatched his glasses off and barked, "*Ysh!mqvad.*"

And Michael Ryan put himself between us.

"You heard the lady," he said. Very quiet, very cold. "You need to leave now."

"Not without what's mine!"

Michael took half a step forward. Now it was Osborne who backed away. "I won't ask nicely again."

Osborne glanced at me, jammed the glasses back on his face, spun and stamped out of the house. On the front porch, he turned back for a moment. "This is not over," he said. But he went on down the three stairs from the porch to the sidewalk, and seconds later I heard his car starting.

My knees were quivering. I sat down, possibly a little faster than was consistent with being calm and in perfect control. "You didn't have to do that," I said.

Michael's lips twitched. "Pure self-interest," he said. "I had a feeling you were about to haul out your cannon again."

"What do you have against guns?" I asked.

"Handled by people who know what they're doing? Nothing. Pulled out by frightened householders? A danger to society."

"I took all the required courses," I told him. "Put in my range time, qualified on my weapon and I have a concealed carry license."

"Mm-hmm. And just how long has it been since you qualified?"

"Umm… eight years," I admitted.

"There you are. People who think they know what they're doing," Michael informed me, "are more dangerous than the ones who know their own ignorance. Come out to Red's with me tomorrow afternoon?"

I blinked, taken aback by the sudden turnaround. "The indoor range place in Pflugerville? Why?"

"For my peace of mind. If I have to live in the same house as a woman who solves problems with a .38 Special, I want to be assured that she knows what she's doing and is up to date on her qualifications. Come on," he said impatiently, "it won't hurt, and there's a great sports bar nearby. We can go for burgers and onion rings afterwards. I'll even buy you a beer."

"How does any woman ever withstand your eloquent invitations? Okay, you're on – and I'll show you that I'm not as bad a shot as you think."

Osborne folded and re-folded the sheet of yellow lined paper that he'd removed from Sienna Brown's leather folder when she left it for a moment at the coffee shop. It was completely damming, made a mockery of her claim to know nothing. The entire page was covered with her scribblings in German script. They didn't make any sense; she started with raving about Jesus and ended with "The relationship between God and man is not a *quid pro quo* transaction, you idiot!"

A religious maniac? Oh well, it didn't matter. The important thing was that she wrote German script; ergo, she could read those notes Koshan Idrisov had been hawking as well as he could.

And the very last word on the page – *ysh!mqvad* – was too like the phrase he'd learned from Idrisov for coincidence – oh, not literally like it, but in form and style it had to be another word of Alt-Shaimaki. He wondered what it did. Nothing much, to judge from his experience in the living room.

He still had those three scans that Jackson had pulled off Idrisov's laptop and printed out for him. The logical next step was to go through those and see if he could find any more phrases of power, anything to give him an edge against this sassy young woman. What a pity she hadn't turned out to be the frail old lady he'd imagined Idrisov's landlady to be! *This* one, armed with the gun the P.I. had reported, could be trouble.

He'd just have to use Alt-Shaimaki to get control of her, make her give up the papers she had clearly stolen from Idrisov and hidden for her own profit.

Or... maybe he could use other resources to get the papers without personally appearing in the matter. Little Mira Martinez probably knew the right sort of people, and she was as dependent on him for dissertation approval as Carrie Jackson.

He didn't *have* to make Sienna Brown disappear, though in the long run it might be the only way to deal with an inconvenient woman who knew too much about the Language.

Anyway, it would be a mistake to go that far before he had his hands on the actual papers.

9. The projectile is accurate

"Do you need to take a break and get a cup of coffee? You're not going to hit anything if you can't open your eyes wide enough to see the target."

"I'm *fine*," I told the annoying man. Who died and made him my own personal gadfly, anyway? I might have been up a bit later than I'd planned last night. My eyes might be slightly tired from poring over that blasted notebook by lamplight last night and by daylight all morning. But I was perfectly well able to hit a target at an indoor shooting range. It was just a matter of awakening the muscle memory from the lessons and range time I'd put in eight years ago. Wasn't it? And if it wasn't, well, Koshan's notebook had suggested a little fix for that problem. Not that I believed for one minute it would work; Laura had been right, there was no such thing as magic. Still, I did remember the relevant words. Just in case. "Let's get this over with."

"Ah, yes. Just the attitude I like to see in women I ask out."

"Maybe you should consider more romantic destinations than Red's."

I put on the ear protectors, loaded my gun and took up a standard shooting stance, prepared to blow the paper target...

Well, hell. I had at least expected to place some holes in the thing! I'd been able to do that much after the lessons, hadn't I?

Michael's mouth was moving. When wasn't it? I pushed the ear protectors off.

"If I'd known you were *that* bad," he said, "I'd have been more frightened, the other night, when you stopped aiming at me. That would have been when I was really in danger."

"It's just a… a knack. I'm out of practice."

"You sure are!"

I glowered at him. "Like you could do so much better?"

"I thought you'd never ask."

I for sure hadn't expected him to put a super-close grouping in the center of the damned target.

"Your turn," he said. "But your stance is all wrong."

I gave him a dirty look and prepared to make my own grouping just as close to the center.

Well, okay. At least this time I winged the target.

"Hot shot," he jeered. "You've got that piece of paper running scared now. Look, you need to get your wrists up more."

Without even asking permission, he stepped behind me and slipped his hands under my wrists. He was tall enough to make it work.

I started feeling shaky. There's nothing remotely erotic about the atmosphere of a shooting range. All the same, I was reacting in a way I didn't really like to the closeness of his body.

Or maybe I liked it too well. Whatever: time to put an end to this. I shook his hands off. "Don't distract me." Under my breath, I muttered, "*Dzhla#m qto! ghri.*" My vision darkened until all I saw clearly was the target, and I felt invisible forces pulling me as if to draw me into a spiraling path down the cone of light that led to that little piece of paper. Taking a deep breath, I braced my feet and took aim for my third go at a distant target.

I winced with pain as the gun went off. Suddenly I might as well not have been wearing the earmuffs at all. I squeezed my eyes shut against the stabbing pain and pulled the trigger five more times.

"How did you *do* that?" Michael's tone conveyed equal parts amazement and respect. I squinted at the target that came back to me. Nice. Tight. Grouping. Just like I'd expected to do on the first round.

"Told you I wasn't that bad, didn't I? But my head's killing me. Can we go now?"

He actually looked worried as we left the shooting range. "You're awfully pale. What happened?"

"Migraine," I managed.

"That happen often? With no warning?"

Not before this last week or so, it hadn't. I shrugged. "Maybe Austin has found one more weed that I'm allergic to. It happens."

"Want me to take you straight home?"

I would have shaken my head, but didn't want to risk it. "I'm hungry. You know a nice *dark* sports bar?"

"My favorite kind," he said, cheering up, "especially when I'm with a pretty girl."

"Who just happens to be a very good shot."

"I, ah, wasn't thinking so much about that part."

The place he took me to was not only dark, it was also cool and – after he persuaded the proprietor to turn the TV down – quiet. That, plus food, plus caffeine in the form of a Diet Coke, alleviated the headache remarkably fast. The only problem was, I felt oddly confused. I stared into Michael's eyes and tried to make sense of what he was saying.

"Don't you think so?"

I had to confess that I hadn't been listening. "I said," he repeated impatiently, "that Osborne guy is bad news. And you're in a bad position now, because he obviously doesn't believe that you aren't concealing Koshan Idrisov's papers. He'll be back for another try, and I can't guard the house 24/7."

"You don't need to," I said. "I can take care of myself." That had been the whole point of this trip to the indoor shooting range in Pflugerville. Hadn't it?

"You'll be safer," he said, "if you just give me whatever you're hiding. I can let him know I have it, and that'll focus his attention on me instead of you."

It was actually a tempting suggestion. But I wasn't through studying the notebook yet. All I'd done so far was skim through the notes, getting a feel for the language without doing any formal analysis. If I could just have one reasonably quiet day without people demanding things of me, without confrontations and shooting practice and headaches, maybe I could…

could… Could what? It was hard to concentrate. I couldn't even quite remember what Michael had just said. I blinked and tried to focus.

"You want me to give you something?"

"The notebook! Before Osborne steals it from you, and quite likely hurts you in the process."

I considered that through my haze of confusion and fuzzy memories. Had I ever told Michael about that stained, perfect-bound ledger I'd found when stripping the bed in Koshan's room? I must have; how else would have he have known about it? Still, I tried to stall.

Eins, zwei, drei… "What notebook?"

"Oh, I think you know what I'm talking about," he said. Quiet, but with the same hint of steel in his voice that had been evident when he told Dr. Osborne to get out of the house.

I concentrated on my burger to give myself some time. "Nope," I said when I'd counted to ten in Latin and reduced the burger to a sliver of crust and some limp lettuce. "I don't know. Haven't a clue."

"Do you *want* that maniac to come after you again?"

I trailed a stray French fry through the ketchup on my plate. "You are talking about a highly respected tenured professor with more publications than I've had real estate closings."

"To hell with his publication history. Did you look at his *eyes?*"

I shivered involuntarily, took a long swig of my beer to conceal the reaction. Yes, the highly respected professor had wild eyes behind those square spectacles. "He's always been kind of strange," I admitted. "But that has nothing to do with me. Ten years ago his grad students used to say that if he took his glasses off, it was time to run."

"But you're not running."

Sowo, tali, tsoi. I can actually count up to nine in Cherokee, but this was the first time I'd found one-third of my vocabulary useful. "I don't have anything he could possibly be interested in. I'm sure he'll come to his senses and realize that soon, and then he won't be a problem any longer."

"Sienna Brown," Michael said, "has anybody ever told you that you are a *really bad* liar?"

Actually, Laura had touched on that once or twice. I just figured it was part of my general social ineptitude package. But with Michael Ryan's blue eyes drilling into mine, it seemed like more of a problem than I'd thought before.

"It's getting late," I said. I must have lost track of time; it was dark outside already. "Take me home."

There weren't any parking places left outside my house. "I'll let you off here and go find somewhere to park," Michael suggested. Sounded reasonable to me. I stepped out into the warm, soft darkness of an Austin summer evening. Street lighting on my block wasn't great, but you didn't really need it in the summer; the light from other people's houses and screen porches was enough to go by.

It was, for instance, enough to show the gang-style tattoos on the fat guy who came barreling out of my front door and knocked me down. Laura followed him, screaming. He exhibited a surprising turn of speed, rounding the corner before I'd done more than pick myself up. "Get him!" Laura panted. "He took your real estate notebook!"

I saw red.

Then I saw lights; Michael, still driving, had pulled up in front of the house for the second time. I jumped into the passenger seat and pointed in the direction the fat guy had disappeared into. Something about that outline had been extremely familiar... Michael stood on the gas and screeched around the corner. Nobody was visible, but the shaking of branches showed where someone had just been.

"Down the alley!" I gasped. The car slewed around and went bucketing along the narrow alley behind the houses. I saw a bulky shape several houses away, screamed and pointed. Just before the intruder reached a cross street, Laura's little Audi pulled across the alley and the guy thudded into the side of her car, unable to stop in time. I leapt out of Michael's car and threw myself on him. Yep – a very familiar outline.

"Sammy Martinez, what the *hell* are you doing breaking into my house?" I demanded.

Michael's car crept towards us and the headlights shone on the unlovely sight of an overweight, sweaty young man wearing a wife-beater T-shirt and two full sleeves of what looked like gang tattoos. "And what's with all the ink?" I added.

"Rub-on… rub off," Sammy panted.

Michael got out of his car without turning off the lights. His shadow fell across Sammy. "You know this son of a bitch?"

"I took Accelerated Russian with his big sister. Mira Martinez." I turned back to Sammy and snatched my precious folder out of his hand. "Give me that! What the hell did you think you were doing?"

Rather than answering directly, Sammy scrubbed at one shoulder. "See? They come off."

Yes. I could see the heavy black-letter "13" starting to peel away from his skin. And below that I could see some long, angry welts. It appeared that Cath Palug hadn't approved of the invasion.

"Halloween isn't for two months yet. And if you'd been caught by somebody who didn't happen to like your big sister, I don't think the cops would have taken rub-off tattoos as proof of your innocence. Especially after that mess when you were in high school. Once again, Sammy, what the *hell* were you up to?"

"I did it for Mira," Sammy said.

It was the kind of answer that led to all of us sitting around the kitchen table, digging into ice cream while Sammy scrubbed off his temporary gang tats with a paper towel – using up most of my nail polish remover in the process– and I applied antibiotic cream and bandages to the claw marks on his arm.

"Mira's about to get her Ph.D," he said proudly. "But her major professor's one weird dude. He wanted her to, get this, hook him up with some really bad drug cartel dudes."

"*Mira?*"

"He thinks anybody with a Hispanic last name is just one step removed from the cartels. She said Dr. Osborne—"

I groaned.

"See?" Michael said in an undertone. "I told you that guy was trouble."

"Dr. Osborne told her that an ex-student had stolen some notes from him, and he didn't want to get the girl in trouble with the police, he just wanted his papers back. He wanted her to get him in contact with somebody who could scare her into giving them back."

I choked. "*You*, Sammy?" He was older now, but I couldn't quite erase my memory of him as Mira's bumbling little brother who'd been big enough for high school sports but too fat to play well. It still seemed appropriate.

"Hey. I'm big," he said defensively. "And I spent twenty bucks on the baddest temp tattoos you ever seen. What do I do now?"

I lifted the folder I'd taken from him back in the alley. It was the first time Michael had seen it in the light. Why, I wondered, did he look so disappointed? "How about I write you a note for him?"

I was in a really good mood after retrieving my brown leather real estate folder. Aunt Georgia had given it to me when I got my license. It was the most luxurious piece of office equipment I ever expected to own, soft brown suede with my name engraved on it in gold letters, opening out with a slot to hold a yellow pad and flat pockets for my bits and pieces of paperwork. Even if most of that "paperwork" was done on my phone nowadays, I treasured the gift.

Now I tore off the page of notes about starter homes from Hutto to San Marcos and scribbled quickly on a fresh sheet of paper, reading aloud as I did so: "Dear Dr. Osborne, I do not have whatever it is you are looking for. Please quit sending people to steal my things. The notebook your drug cartel henchman almost succeeded in taking was a gift from my aunt and I will not hesitate to involve the police if anybody goes after it again. Yours, Sienna Brown." I signed my name with a defiant flourish, tore out the page and handed it to Sammy.

"Hey, cool. You didn't give me away!" he exclaimed in delight.

"I wouldn't want to make trouble for Mira."

10. I worked for a living

When Sammy departed, the two women washed up the ice cream bowls and Sienna disappeared into Laura's side of the house. Michael could just hear the murmur of their conversation from where he sat in the kitchen.

He went out onto the spacious front porch. The glider was in front of Laura Jacobson's spare-room windows; he moved over to the far side of the porch and sat on the floor. From here he could see the two women silhouetted against the light and would be warned if they broke off their chat, but they – if he kept his voice down – wouldn't be able to hear him on the phone.

It would have been smarter to call from somewhere else, but he didn't like the idea of leaving them alone in the house. The next person that professor sent might not be a bumbling fool.

"Hank," he said, "we need to talk. This, this job… isn't shaking out the way we thought it would. I'm not sure I can do what you want."

"Son, my previous experience with you suggests you can do just about anything you want. What's the hold-up?"

"Maybe," Michael said, surprising himself, "maybe I don't want to do this job. She's… not what I expected."

"What's that got to do with anything? The *notes* are what matter to me."

"Yes. Well… Had you considered just telling her the truth?"

"You think she's that easy to con?"

"I said, the *truth*," Michael snapped impatiently. "Tell her you really, really want to know all about this mysterious language that isn't anything like, like…" He groped for the names Hank had used when they planned this op.

72

"Tazakh or Khaklan or Uugie."

"You mean, Taklan or Kazakh or Uighur."

"*Whatever*. And when did you become an expert on Central Asian languages, anyway?"

"I'm not," Hank said, "not yet. But I went to Taklanistan when I was younger, I have heard the stories about Shaimak, and young Idrisov showed me... some real interesting things. Ryan, I need that notebook. The one with the page Idrisov copied."

"She insists she doesn't have a notebook," Michael said, "and after tonight, I halfway believe her! This dope the professor sent to steal it, all he could find was the leather folder where she keeps her real estate papers – and she got that back."

"Well, tell the half of you that doesn't believe her yet to keep on looking."

"*I'm tired of lying to her*," Michael said between his teeth. "She's smart and spunky and..."

Hank cut him off with an aggrieved sigh. "I thought I could count on you not to mess up the job by falling in love. Just because the person hiding the notes happens to be a pretty girl..."

"She's not! I mean, I'm not! It's, it's just..."

"Not pretty?"

"No," Michael said. She wasn't. Big mouth, firm chin, straight dark brows; not exactly a recipe for beauty. Except when she was scribbling that defiant note to Osborne, and then she'd been – not pretty, no, but *something*: brown eyes snapping with amber fire, and all that reddish-brown hair bursting loose to frame her face, and... And that had nothing to do with the problem.

"If I could just explain to her *why* you want the information so badly..." he tried again.

"You can't, because she wouldn't believe it."

"No – I can't because you haven't told me!"

"Well, you wouldn't believe it either."

"I need to know more," Michael said firmly. "What you've told me so far doesn't account for what's been happening."

"You'd be amazed," Hank said, "what lengths people in academia will go to just to get one step ahead of their competition. You know what they say about conflicts in that world: they're so bitter because the stakes are so small."

"You are not in that world," Michael pointed out. "Or are you thinking that being the discoverer of a hitherto undocumented language will turn you into a respected scholar? I don't think so. Not when you won't be able to explain where you got the notes on that language. You can't publish."

Hank sighed. "No. Believe you me, I do not want to publish those notes. That would be the worst possible outcome. Michael… you can't quit, okay? Not yet. Give me a few days to work something out. But for now, you're the only person in a position to keep Ed Osborne out of the loop. Trust me, it would be a calamity for him to get his mitts on them."

"Although you won't tell me why."

"Just stay there. Watch what happens. And protect…"

"Protect the girl from him?"

"Oh, yes, yes, of course. And protect the *data*."

It was an unsatisfactory note on which to end the conversation, but the women indoors were getting up. The lights in Laura's front room went off and Sienna came out and sank into the glider on the porch.

***

Laura hadn't been any more help straightening out my feelings than she had been the last time we talked. To begin with, she was still adamant that I was imagining the strange events around the language in the notebook.

"It's happened two times now," I insisted. "That first time, I used a sentence meaning that my clients were happy; they made an offer on the property they were looking at; and I got a migraine."

"Both of which," Laura scoffed, "are such highly unusual events. Sienna, you're a realtor; if you don't expect your clients ever to make an offer, then aren't you in the wrong business?"

"You'd be surprised," I said darkly. "Far too often that expectation is the triumph of hope over experience. This was a *very good* offer, and one that five minutes earlier Bruce Sutherland had been resisting."

Laura shrugged. "Haven't we been over that? His wife wanted the place, and you probably overcame his resistance with one of your charm offensives. You can be charming, Sienna, you know that."

"Not," I said, reflecting on other recent events, "with men I'm interested in."

"No," Laura agreed, "you tend to freeze them out. I've been wondering when that would change. So you're reciprocating this guy Michael's interest? Is that what's spooked you?"

"No! I mean, I'm not – and anyway, he's not – and – oh, I need to tell you about the other thing. We went to Red's this afternoon, and the same thing happened."

"What, he made an offer on one of your listings?"

"Don't give me a hard time, you know that's not what I meant. I used *that language* again – I wasn't doing so well at the range, I'm out of practice and he was teasing me about it. I used a sentence that meant something like, 'The projectile is thrown accurately,' and I got a perfect grouping at the center of the target, and my head started hurting."

Laura giggled. "So you lost your temper, forgot to be nervous, and your aim improved. And you got a headache while you were hanging out at a place full of loud noises and smelling like gunpowder. Oh, yes – clear evidence of witchcraft! You're lucky nobody tried to duck you in a stock tank! Sienna, it's perfectly clear what's really going on with you, and it's nothing supernatural."

"It isn't?" At that point I would have been happy with any alternative explanation.

"Not in the least. You, my girl, have a bad case of Michael Ryan."

Make that *almost* any alternative.

"What? I do not! He's the most annoying man I've ever met!"

"I guess that's one way of describing his effect on you," Laura said with a sly grin. "What's so terrible about admitting it? He's cute, personable—"

"He's a man of mystery. I don't know why he finagled his way into renting my spare room or what he's really doing here."

"Uh-huh. That adds to his charm, doesn't it? Handsome mystery man who's obviously crazy about you. Maybe just once, Sienna, you could allow yourself to go for it without dotting all the i's and crossing all the t's?"

"I did that once. It was the worst mistake of my life."

"No, you let somebody else push you into doubting your own judgment. Very different."

I didn't want to go over the squalid details of that long-past episode. "Well, he's pushy too. Michael is." I told her about his comments when we'd been watching *Gaslight* the day before.

"It sounds to me," said the provoking woman, "as though he's been a perfect gentleman and you're letting yourself be spooked by your own feelings."

"You," I told her, "are a hopeless romantic."

"I'm a *sleepy* romantic," Laura said with a yawn. "Paco's band closed down the White Horse last night, I spent half the day working up some new material because they want us back next weekend, and now I've had to deal with a home invasion, a car chase, a wannabe gangbanger and the course of true love."

I was sympathetic right up to that last crack. "Fine, I'll let you sleep in peace." And I stomped off to sit on the front porch glider and rock myself into a semblance of calm before trying to go to sleep. I didn't realize until I had started pushing myself back and forth with one foot that Michael was sitting on the floor in the shadowy far corner of the porch, knees drawn up, back propped against the massive corner pillar. It would be entirely too much trouble to jump up and flounce off for the second time in just ninety seconds, so I kept pushing the glider and hoped he'd have the tact to ignore the regular creaking noise.

I should have known better, of course. "Tact" was a word that didn't belong in the same sentence as "Michael Ryan."

"How's the headache?" he asked just as I was beginning to think we could quietly ignore one another.

"Huh? Oh. Better. Fine, actually." It had come and gone so quickly that it wasn't quite real to me. Strange. My migraines used to be rare, but they hung around for hours. Flash migraines, switching on and off like an electric light, were a new and unsettling development. The possibility of some kind of brain tumor did cross my mind, but it wasn't worth the trouble of worrying about, was it? Besides, my brain was working perfectly fine. I thought. Okay, there'd been a few minutes earlier, at the sports bar, when I'd had some trouble concentrating enough to follow the conversation, but that was just the usual brain fuzz that accompanied a bad headache. I thought.

"I suppose, though, crazy people think they're sane and it's the ones around them who have the problem." I didn't realize until it was too late that I'd voiced the thought.

"Hey," Michael said, sounding pained, "I haven't actually called you crazy since the night we met."

"Does that mean you've been thinking it, and want credit for your verbal self-restraint?"

He sighed. "How about it means just what I said? Sienna, do you always take what people say apart and analyze it syllable by syllable?"

"It's what linguists do. And don't you have anything to think about but my life?"

"At the moment," he said, "I am slightly underemployed."

I rocked back and forth in the glider, considering that statement. Given how much free time he seemed to have to hang around the house, drag me to shooting ranges, and so forth... "'Slightly' might be an understatement. Do you have any kind of a job?"

"Worried about whether I'm good for the rent?"

"We landladies do tend to focus on those unimportant details." Given the amount of cash he'd forked over to Aunt Georgia for the privilege of moving in immediately, his income or lack of one hadn't even crossed my mind. "But no, I was just wondering why you don't come and go at regular hours like a normal person."

"Like you? Or Laura?"

"Point taken. Laura's a singer, she can't be expected to keep normal hours. I'm self-employed as a realtor and language tutor, same thing. What's your excuse?"

"I'm... self-employed... too," he said. He didn't sound all that happy about it.

I waited through half a dozen more swings of the glider. The cicadas that had stopped when I came out onto the porch resumed their regular chirring. The combination could have been a postmodern musical composition: Creaks and Buzzes for Insects and Lawn Furniture. The soft, humid night air brushed my cheek with each movement. It also frizzed up my hair, but thinking about that didn't help me achieve calmness.

"And?"

"And what?"

"And what do you *do*?" I snapped. "For heaven's sake, isn't that what everybody asks everybody else when they first meet socially?"

"I suppose so," he said. "Rather a pity, isn't it? We don't have families or churches or other associations any more; the workplace becomes our identity."

I hadn't exactly signed on for a sophomoric BS discussion. "Well, it's better than nothing."

"Yeah… It used to be enough for me. In my former job."

"Which was?" I was surprised his ability to avoid specifics hadn't re-started my headache. He was certainly aggravating enough.

He shifted position, stretching one leg out in front of him. "I was in the military. Special Forces."

Wow, two whole sentences out of the Man of Mystery. "You were?"

"What, that's so surprising?"

"You just didn't seem like a military type."

"Too flexible, too creative?"

"Too *irritating*. And if you're so used to the army, how come you turned white when I pointed a gun at you?"

He chuckled, a low sound blending in with the buzzing of the cicadas. "I knew what a .38 can do to the human body, and I didn't know whether you were scared enough to pull the trigger without provocation. Since I left the Service I haven't generally had to worry about crazed civilians randomly shooting me."

"That wouldn't have been random," I defended myself, "it would have been a perfectly reasonable response to an intruder in my bathroom. Were you this argumentative in the army?"

"That was mentioned occasionally by my superior officers. I served for eight years, but the consensus of opinion was that my attitude was not consistent with a long-term career in the armed forces."

"I can see how the other officers might have felt that way."

"Oh, I wasn't an officer, I worked for a living. NCO."

For him, I guessed, that was the equivalent of a detailed resumé. But I felt I could stand to hear a few more details.

"Where did you serve?"

"Our AO – area of operations – was officially Africa, but we spent a lot of time in Afghanistan... I learned plenty, but not the sort of skills that automatically transfer to an interesting civilian job."

"So what was next? Private security?"

"I actually wanted to get out of the shooting-people line of work altogether. Unfortunately, there aren't a lot of nice peaceful civilian jobs just crying out for someone who can field-strip a Barrett M107 blindfolded or take a head shot at 1200 yards."

I had no idea what the first qualification even meant, but it sounded impressive. Probably not a big hit in the business world, though. "I know what that's like... sort of. I mean, not the specifics, but I managed to graduate with a whole lot of skills that it turns out aren't highly in demand. At least not in America, where people will go to any length to avoid foreign languages. I read German, French, Spanish, Russian and Italian; I know enough Arabic to bargain for a Berber rug in Marrakesh and I can make polite conversation in Farsi." I had just enough sense to stop there. The man didn't want to know even that much about my linguistic abilities; he certainly wouldn't be interested in a list of all the other bits and pieces of languages that had rubbed off on me over the years. There were a lot of them; I'm not good at small talk, so if I'm in the same room with somebody who speaks a language I don't know I get them to teach me a few words. You wouldn't believe how many ways I can count to ten.

"You're better off than I am," Michael grumbled, "at least your random skills don't involve killing people."

"Funny, I was just thinking the opposite. I mean, nobody's invited me to tea in Tehran or flown me to Morocco to go shopping, and I'm not holding my breath waiting for that to happen. Whereas sometimes people *want* other people killed, and I'm told they're willing to pay quite a lot for the service."

"Yeah, well, apart from wanting to get out of that line of work, it's immoral and illegal. I don't see myself building a career as a hit man, Sienna."

I was unwilling to concede in this particular game of Life Failure. "I'm sure there are other skills you developed in the army that could be useful in civilian life."

"Oh, sure. I'm just having trouble thinking of any Special Forces experience that applies to my current life issues." He gave me an intense stare suggesting that I was among those issues. "After all, it's not like I can hold a gun on you to get a goodnight kiss."

I gasped. His stare intensified. "Would anything less work?"

It wasn't that much trouble to get up and go inside, after all.

Getting to sleep was a different story, though.

11. Real estate agents and danger

The final program in this year's Continuing Education requirement was a seminar on "Real Estate Agents and Danger." After my recent experiences, the title spoke to me. I showed up with a clean yellow pad, two fresh pens, and a positive attitude, prepared to take notes. And it was a good thing, because there were only seven attendees besides Carly, Davis and me. I would have to look attentive; no handy crowd to hide behind this time. Sadly, most of the speakers covered very old, familiar ground, and none of them addressed such hot topics as people breaking into your house to steal an ex-tenant's possessions, being injured by the backlash from using magic to influence clients, or having once-respected scholars trying to hire someone from a drug cartel to steal your papers.

The fact that Dr. Osborne had failed ludicrously in that last attempt didn't make him innocent in my eyes, just incompetent. And I didn't feel at all sure that I could count on the continued incompetence of someone who'd achieved both tenure and the Hedin Chair in Central Asian Linguistics before he was forty. Dr. Osborne had been swimming in the piranha-infested waters of faculty politics since before I knew the difference between a cognate and a loan-word, and I didn't kid myself: in that environment, I was a minnow and he was a shark. When he got his bearings, I would be *lunch*. Okay, the metaphor may not be totally biologically coherent, but you get the idea.

He might be searching the house at this very moment. I hadn't exactly found the most ingenious hiding place for Koshan's notebook before dashing off to make it to this seminar on time. Well, too late to worry about that now.

On the bright side, if he did get into the house and found the notebook, he would presumably stop harassing me.

To keep my mind from wandering while the speakers went over the tried and true, I promised myself that I would write down any safety tips that I hadn't already internalized.

"Ask a lot of questions and listen to the answers."

"Ask for ID."

"Don't meet clients at the office if you're going to be the only one there."

Aunt Georgia had *paid* for us to listen to these nuggets of received wisdom? This wasn't going to work. Maybe I should scribble down a one-sentence summary of every tip without evaluating it.

"Call 911 if you feel yourself in danger; don't be shy." Shy, ha! The only reason I hadn't called 911 when I thought Michael Ryan was a burglar was because that darned face-recognition app on my phone hadn't recognized me. True, Laura had pointed out later that most cell phones let you call 911 even if you weren't logged in, but who thinks about things like that when you're terrified?

After the way we'd parted last night, thinking about Michael and how scared I'd been was like rubbing a sore spot to verify that yes, you did have a nasty bruise there. *Concentrate*, Sienna!

"Don't wear expensive jewelry to work." Not a problem for me. I slid a covert glance over at Carly, but she was turning her wrist and admiring her designer wristwatch in the light. So, not a problem for her either, in a different sense: she wasn't likely to give up wearing that status symbol just because somebody might want to steal it from her. Carly might not be my favorite person, but she was tough. I wondered how she would deal with something like Koshan's explosive notebook.

"Act confident and strong, don't give the impression of being a victim." Carly had that one covered too. As for Davis, all he needed to do was flex a few of his impressive muscles. What about me, did I come across like a potential victim? I shook my head. I might not look like a professional athlete, but I stood 5'9" in flats and I wasn't exactly fragile.

"Miss Brown, you had a comment?"

I blinked and mentally replayed the last few seconds. By the time I started wondering if Dr. Osborne saw me as an easy victim, the speaker had already moved on to warning us about the dangers of hosting open houses alone.

"No – no, I was just, uh, just trying to get my pen to flow." I tapped it vigorously on the yellow pad to demonstrate and was rewarded by a dime-sized blotch of oily black ink. Damn! If that overflowed onto my lap or rubbed off on my hands, this beige linen suit was a goner. I tore off the page and started folding it up, very carefully.

"I did," said Carly, and I blinked in surprise. It wasn't exactly standard procedure for her to come to my rescue in situations like this.

"Miss Gordon?"

"Oh, call me Carly." She dimpled at the speaker and he blinked. That smile of hers *was* dazzling – at least until you noticed the slightly too-long incisors and began looking for the telltale trickle of blood.

What? I never said I'm not catty. At least give me this much credit, I'm the same person on the surface as I am inside; I never pretended to be a compendium of all the virtues.

"I just wanted to say," Carly began, breathily, "how very wise you are to insist that a woman not try to show an open house on her own…"

I'd thought that advice applied to all agents. But to be fair, women probably were more at risk than men in that situation.

"It can be…" Her voice died down as though she found it impossibly painful to speak. "Trouble… I've learned that for myself." Now she sounded as though she might start to cry.

"Were there any aspects of that experience you'd like to share with the class?"

"No – no, I just wanted to say that it's not much fun being cornered." She sighed deeply. "I hope no one here – no one else – has to learn that the hard way."

Christ, I hoped so too. Carly was still not my favorite person, but I'd never guessed that a trauma like that might underly her sometimes abrasive personality.

I said as much to Davis when we were milling around during a very short lunch break – they'd advertised lunch as covered within the seminar cost, and then they brought in pre-packaged sandwiches and little airline-type bags of pretzels – and he laughed quietly. "Don't waste too much sympathy. I was around when Carly had that 'traumatic experience' – we were both working for a local branch of 21 Realty then – and in her first version, she was royally pissed off because some guy who didn't meet her standards had the nerve to ask her out. It didn't become a frightening encounter with a pushy would-be date until a year later, and she's been polishing it up and adding Gothic shadows and date-rape penumbras ever since then."

I stopped empathizing with Carly and switched over to describing interesting executions for her during the second half of the seminar. (What? No, of course I wasn't writing those notes in English for anybody to read over my shoulder. I was writing French text in German script. I like my privacy.)

Between Michael last night and Carly today, I felt as if a layer of my skin had been sandpapered off. Instead of joining the panelists and the rest of the class for a drink after the session ended early, I headed straight home. Aunt Georgia could lecture me about building a social life to build a client list some other day. Better yet, she could lecture Carly, who did everything by the book and still, to her puzzlement, didn't bring in a lot more clients than I did. One of those things that convinced Carly there was a long-term misalignment in the Force, some dark powers denying her the success she deserved.

***

Michael had nothing in particular against his landlady's other tenant, Laura Jacobson, but he did feel that having to work around *two* unpredictable females with different and very fluid schedules – if you could even use that term for the way the women ambled through their days – created one of the more challenging environments he'd encountered in two years of finding unusual curios that Hank Henderson wanted tracked down. By contrast, infiltrating the cartels that had cornered a collection of pre-Columbian antiquities while trying to take over Phoenix had been positively restful. So had his undercover investigation of a corrupt police force in a California bedroom suburb, where some very ugly and very rare Chinese statuettes had fallen foul of their theories on civil forfeiture. In both those cases he hadn't had to worry about hurt feelings or misunderstandings or any of that touchy-feely stuff. Try not to get caught, be prepared to shoot your way out of trouble, and remember that if you screw up you won't live long enough to worry about it; that was the kind of assignment he felt comfortable with.

Not so different from his time in the army, that way. Hmm. When he was discharged he'd vowed never to do that again. But had he unconsciously gravitated back towards what was familiar, the long periods of waiting interspersed with the quick violence?

And was that what had appealed to the eccentric Henderson about him – the potential for violence? And if so, what the hell was he doing on a job that involved going through a girl's lingerie drawers – or that would do so, if both the idiot females would just leave the house *at the same time*?

It was the kind of question that hadn't troubled him before, the sort of thing a man wouldn't think about unless he'd been trapped for far too long in some female-dominated world where people sat around eating crazy mixes of ice cream flavors and analyzing their feelings and other people's words in way too much detail. Had he really only been working this case for two weeks? This morning, while he cracked his knuckles and waited for Laura Jacobson to go somewhere so he could take advantage of Sienna's being stuck in a day-long seminar… this one morning already felt like it had lasted a month.

The blasted woman had slept so late, at ten o'clock he'd decided she was going to sleep all day and he might as well get on with searching Sienna's room.

At ten-oh-five, naturally, Laura started fluttering around, spilling coffee on her fluffy robe and raising a screech that had him pounding into the kitchen, ready to repel marauders. Then she'd had him holding the stained sleeve while she poured water on it, then she'd insisted on fixing him a cup of coffee to thank him for his help, then she'd perched on the kitchen table and explained how she never ever ate breakfast… while going through an amazing quantity of cold leftover pizza.

For two more hours she'd driven him crazy by popping up here and there without warning. In Sienna's room to borrow a crimson silk scarf, in the living room for an interminable rambling cell phone call 'because the signal's better here,' then squeaking and disappearing into her own rooms when some long-haired musician clomped in.

She'd gone back and forth between dressing to go out and arguing something about a band with the musician. The whole discussion was so loaded with phrases like "dancy vibes," and "backbeat" and "interesting harmonics" that Michael didn't even try to follow it; he just slumped against the headboard of his bed, playing a game on his phone and waiting for them to get on with it and go out to lunch.

Preferably before dinner.

Finally – after another interminable multi-party phone call in which apparently the whole band had to debate the virtues of three different Tex-Mex restaurants – Laura and her musician friend drifted out of the house, reminding Michael to be sure and lock up if he went anywhere because somebody might try to get in again.

He promised faithfully to lock up against unauthorized entrants, and didn't even feel slightly hypocritical in doing so. After all, he didn't want Edward Osborne getting hold of that notebook Sienna was obviously hiding somewhere. Not first, anyway.

Stealing from Sienna: that made him more uncomfortable the better he got to know her. Or maybe the real problem was, the better he *wanted* to get to know her. Here he was on one hand trying to get her to relax, let go of her skittish ways and trust him – and on the other, he was being about as low and untrustworthy as anybody could be. He'd thought of a compromise and prepared to implement it, but wasn't sure that would salve his conscience adequately.

Even that compromise, though, did require him to get his mitts on that notebook full of information in German script. Analysis of the scan fragment Henderson held suggested it wasn't a standard-size American notebook, but something tall and skinny. Maybe a standard *German* size? And it was perfect-bound; one side of the scan showed the lines of stitching that held the narrow pages in place. So, an unusual little notebook, probably in an unusual place.

He didn't even have to pick the lock on Sienna's bedroom door; she must have rushed off that morning without locking it. Maybe she never did lock it. He didn't know much about her, did he? He pushed the door open, stepped inside softly – and his foot came down on a squashy thing that howled like a banshee, raked his ankle with a set of razor-sharp spikes, bounced off the far wall and landed on top of a tall bookcase from which it treated him to a series of menacing hisses.

"What the fuck are you, cat, the demon guardian of the lady's privacy?" Michael demanded *sotto voce*.

The monster cat with the Welsh name didn't answer him, but it did stop hissing. And in the silence he could hear an ominous dripping. Oh, *hell*. Apparently the blasted woman couldn't just keep a glass of water beside the bed; she kept a huge bottle marked with hours of the day, as if drinking water were a homework assignment.

And right now half of that assignment was puddling on the floor, while the other half soaked into the mattress. Chance that she wouldn't notice anything: nil. Well, he'd worry about that later. First he had to set up his escape plan. He relocked the door behind him, so that he'd have a few seconds warning if she came back, drew the bolts on both bathroom doors and opened them so he could beat it out that way.

He figured she was the kind of idiot who'd keep her gun under the pillow. If it got soaked he'd be that much ahead, but... No luck. No gun. He shoved the pillow out of his way, trying to ignore the hint of Sienna-and-perfume that it gave off, and slipped his hands between the mattress and box spring. No gun there either, but he felt something else – something flat, rectangular and rigid. Was this it? He drew out a battered composition book – tall and skinny, matching the dimensions they'd deduced from the scan fragment, with a mostly-green cover stained by unidentifiable substances. Flipped it open and nodded at the sight of a spiky handwriting filling the pages. A perfect match for the sample.

Not bad! At the cost of a little blood and an adrenaline burst when that cat-monster exploded, he'd found his prize almost at once.

Michael glanced at the low dresser beside the bed. Apart from the upset water bottle, it was covered with women's trivia: bottles of scent and lotion, hairpins and creased ribbons, three kinds of combs, why did anybody need three combs with different sized teeth, for heaven's sake? He told himself he was lucky not to have to search the dresser, Sienna was clearly a slob and he had already learned that the homes of people like that were the hardest to search unnoticeably. In place of a simple rule like "A place for everything and everything in its place," they substituted a photographic memory for where they'd dropped every little thing, and heaven help you if you disturbed the arrangement!

The drawers were probably just as much of a disaster as the top of the dresser, and he was *lucky* that he wasn't forced to slide them open and fill his hands with silky lingerie and semi-transparent nightgowns like the one she'd been wearing that first night and, and, damn it! He was *not* having some kind of perverted fantasy about invading the privacy of a woman he barely knew. And who was unbelievably skittish about her privacy.

Not.

He took the notebook through the bathroom and into his own room, which got better light at this time of day, and where it was easier to focus. He stacked the cardboard boxes holding the rest of Koshan Idrisov's possessions to make a convenient stand beside the side window, opened the notebook, weighed the corners of the pages down with his phone and car keys, and got to work with a very small camera adapted to low light conditions and capable of super-mega-pixel resolution. That had been a necessary investment; if he wanted Hank to accept photographs instead of the originals, he wanted to offer him superb images, not just cell phone snapshots.

There was a daunting amount of material to photograph, and the job couldn't be rushed. He was sweating lightly by the time he got to the last page, where the foreign writing trailed down across the paper as if the writer were dying. Perhaps he had been, at that; the provenance of this notebook was among the many things Hank had managed not to tell him about this job.

Four-thirty. Not great, but not terrible. The seminar was supposed to end at five, and she had grumbled something about being expected to go out and be social with everybody afterwards. He probably had a clear hour, hour and a half before he needed to worry about her coming back. As for the Jacobson girl – given the degree of organization she and her friends had displayed earlier, they probably hadn't even agreed on what to order for lunch yet.

In actual fact, he had somewhat less than three minutes. But he didn't learn that until he was bent over Sienna's bed, shoving the notebook back into its hiding place, and the doorknob rattled.

She said something under her breath, and he heard the key in the lock while he was still too many steps from the bathroom door.

12. The wrath of Cath Palug

Funny, I didn't remember locking my bedroom door when I left for the seminar. I supposed I might have done so, though. Given how poorly I'd hidden that blasted notebook, locking the room would have been the smart thing to do. Darn it, I'd meant to put the notebook away in my gun safe, then it had slipped my mind. Maybe I'd been thinking about locking the gun safe and had locked the door instead? Maybe... I jiggled the key in the lock and tried hard to remember having done the same thing early this morning.

I caught my breath as the door swung open. Now *that* I definitely did not remember from this morning. What the hell was Michael Ryan doing there? And behind a locked door, no less. Adrenaline shot through me, making my hands shake. This was like an instant replay of our first meeting. Only worse. This time he was *in my room*, not in a shared bathroom. There could be no good explanation for that. And this time my gun was in the safe where I usually kept it, on the far side of the bed. And on the far side of Michael.

"What are you—" I started to croak. No sound came out. I moistened my lips and tried again. "What the *hell* do you think you're—"

"And cut it out, you damn cat!" he shouted. Apparently he hadn't even noticed me coming in; he was standing with his hands on his hips, yelling up at a yellowish-gray fur shape on top of the bookcase.

"Michael?"

He started and then turned towards me. "*Your* cat," he said, almost snarling, "just peed on my bed. When I tried to throw him out, he ran through the bathroom, jumped on your dresser and slid the length of it.

Knocking all your stuff over."

He moved to give me a view of the dresser. I have to admit that considered in isolation, the top of the dresser looked a lot better than usual; no clutter.

The clutter was distributed over a couple of half-open drawers, the rag rug on the floor, and a corner of my mattress that had apparently just chugged all the water I'd planned to drink that day before I woke late and rushed off without my super-bottle.

I picked my way through the mess, retrieved some expensive cologne, and stoppered the bottle with its remaining quarter-inch of scent.

"Sorry about your perfume," Michael said. "I had no idea the damn cat was going to react that way."

"It's okay," I said absently, "Aunt Georgia gives me a bottle every Christmas. And I'm kind of tired of the scent anyway."

"Well... sorry about *that*, then because I think your room's going to reek of it for a while. But I really can't be expected to herd that cat!"

My knees didn't seem to have got the message that the emergency was over; they were still shaking. I sat down on the edge of the mattress.

It squelched. "How did it absorb all that water so fast?"

"Damned if I know. Maybe this wasn't Caps Lock's first trail of destruction through the room."

"Cath Palug. I didn't mean to lock him in," I said slowly. "Maybe he's annoyed about that. But I don't see how he got into *your* room. I always keep the bathroom door shut and bolted." Since Koshan had moved in, anyway. I'd moved Cath Palug's litter box to the screened back porch where the washer and dryer stood so that I wouldn't have to leave the bathroom door open for him.

Michael shrugged. "Maybe you were in a hurry this morning, forgot. Look, no real harm done. Sorry I yelled at your cat and frightened him into a conniption."

Forgot to bolt the bathroom door?

Forgot that I'd locked the bedroom door?

I shook my head. These memory problems were beginning to worry me. I was forgetting things, losing track of time... I began wondering again about sudden headaches as a symptom of brain damage. Did people under thirty even get brain tumors? Should I make an appointment for an EEG? MRI? Anything? I wasn't even sure what sort of test would be appropriate.

The only thing that was clear to me was that Cath Palug had just created a major laundry chore. "If you'll give me your sheets and quilt, I'll wash them. And get you fresh ones."

He was looking at my face. Too intent; too close. "Is that part of the normal service? You do your tenants' laundry?"

I tried to laugh. It came out wobbly. "Only when my cat is responsible for the damage."

"Well… don't worry about it right now. I've got some other stuff that needs washing, I'll throw it all into the machine in a while." He held out a hand to me. "You don't look so good. I think you should have a nice cup of coffee with lots of sugar."

"Ugh."

"Something else sweet? How about ice cream?"

Now he was talking. Laura and I consider ice cream to be suitable treatment for both shock and suggested brain tumors, not to mention all the other ills that afflict mankind. "There's some Lemon Cheesecake Cookie from Amy's in the freezer."

"You girls eat the damnedest mixtures. What, there's no chocolate in this one?"

"It's a new discovery of Thalia's."

Blank look.

"Friend of mine," I amplified. Of all my tutoring students, Thalia had been memorable for coupling a superb French accent and dazzling intelligence with a total lack of intuition about how the language actually worked. We'd remained friends after she scraped through her second-year French finals – and even after she'd recommended that deadbeat Koshan Idrisov as a tenant. "She just had a baby. She's got this theory that she shouldn't eat chocolate or caffeine while she's nursing." Personally, I didn't see how one could survive caring for a newborn without the support of my good friends Chocolate and Caffeine. Good thing I wasn't the one stuck with the job.

"So, a special mix for nursing mothers?" He took my hand and pulled me to my feet. "Okay, let's see if your other tenant left any in the fridge."

Over a bowl of swirling colors and flavors, ranging from sweet-sharp (lemon) to crunchy vanilla (crushed vanilla Oreos), I began to feel that my brain might resume normal functioning at any minute. Michael barely touched his; he seemed to be more interested in urging me to eat. And the calories did make me feel somewhat more human.

"Don't they feed you at these real estate seminars?"

"Um." Breakfast hadn't happened; I'd awakened too late to do more than throw on my good summer suit, tie my hair back and grab a cup of coffee. That was probably why I'd forgotten to stash the notebook in the gun safe; no need to spin theories about brain damage. Oh well, no harm done. "Packaged sandwiches. Stale. Come to think of it, I threw most of mine away." Maybe that did account for how shaky I was feeling.

I dipped into the luscious mixture again, then looked across the table. "Your ice cream is melting."

"Good," he said without glancing down, "maybe it'll harmonize the clashing flavors."

"Are you one of those people who scorns anything but plain vanilla or plain chocolate?" Thalia told me that she had married a man like that. She said that it did have the upside that he never raided the freezer for her stash of interesting flavors.

"Certainly not," Michael said, sounding offended, "there's also strawberry."

Another man who would pose no danger to a good ice cream stash, then. Not that it necessarily made him a desirable spouse, but in some sense it was a positive quality to stack against all the negative ones I'd already noticed, like being irritating and bossy and unable to let anything go.

"I don't think it was just hunger that shook you up so much just now, though," he went on.

"I wasn't shaky." Well, no more than could be expected after coming home to find my space invaded and my gun out of reach!

"Sienna," he said impatiently, "you should have looked in the mirror. You were so pale your *freckles* looked green."

I mashed the last cookie fragments into the pool of melted lemon cheesecake ice cream and abandoned the bowl to fold my hands on the table. "A gentleman wouldn't comment on my freckles." In summer, particularly after a week at the beach, I liked to believe I had enough of a tan to disguise the sprinkling of little brown spots over the bridge of my nose. That belief saved me the trouble of bothering with makeup; I resented his undermining it.

"I'm not an officer or a gentleman," Michael said, "and I notice things." He put one warm hand over my two cold ones. "Sienna, I wish you'd tell me the truth."

"About what?"

"Well… lots of things. But for starters… Since last night I've been wondering… Sienna. Who *did* hold a gun on you? And how bad was it?"

I stood, picked up our bowls, and turned to set them in the sink.

"Hey," Michael said, "I wasn't finished."

"You are now!" I ran warm water over the melted ice cream.

"No." He stood, behind me. I tensed, but he didn't move around the table to where I was now scouring out the ice cream bowls with scalding hot water and too much detergent on the sponge. "You need to talk to somebody. If it's been eight years and you still go rigid when anybody even hints at it…"

I was surprised. "How did you know it was eight years ago?"

"Just a wild guess. Seemed likely that something happened right before you decided to get your concealed carry license."

I set the clean bowls upside down in the drainer and turned off the water. This time I remembered Aunt Georgia's stalling technique and counted to three before saying anything. *Un, deux, trois…* "Nobody held a gun on me. It wasn't anything like that. I made a stupid mistake, that's all, and I don't particularly like recalling it, and can we talk about something else now? Like how to get the smell of cat urine out of your sheets?"

After listening to Carly this morning, the way she *enjoyed* portraying herself as a victim, I didn't ever want to hear – or tell – another story like that. Which didn't explain, did it, how I wound up sitting down at the kitchen table again. I pulled a loose curl out of the scrunchie that kept the rest of my hair out of my face and twisted it around one finger. And talked. To this man I barely knew. Who, with any luck, would exit my life as swiftly as he'd entered it, so I wouldn't have to look into his eyes and see myself reflected there as a victim… a *stupid* victim.

"It was the middle of my sophomore year," I told him. "I was living here, but not renting rooms; I had the whole house to myself. It had been my parents' house, you know, and Aunt Georgia took care of it after they died, and we thought it would save money if I just lived here when I went to the university…"

And so it had. But the house had also been old, and echoing, and very empty after the previous six years of living in Beeville with Aunt Milly and Uncle Max and my five cousins. In my second year at the university I went to a party, drank far too much, passed out, and when I came to I was back here. In my bedroom. And I wasn't alone.

I never did know his name. He'd told me that I'd invited him to come home with me and that we'd made love before I passed out and it didn't matter that I said I couldn't remember it, I didn't have any right to throw him out now. He was large and acted angry. And I was stupid, and intimidated, and…

"What did he do?"

"Nothing. Nothing more. I mean – I was scared, I locked myself in the bathroom. But I didn't have my phone with me, so I couldn't call anybody. He yelled at me through the door – it seemed to go on for *hours*."

In the morning I ventured into the quiet house and satisfied myself that he was gone. I stayed in the house for three days, taking showers and baths all day every day until the hot water was used up. By then Laura was worried about me, because I never missed Russian Conversation Club on Monday nights, and what was worse, a man I was hand-carrying through his graduate proficiency exams in French saw her on campus and asked why I hadn't met him for our regular tutoring session. She came over and hammered on the door until I let her in.

"She and Aunt Georgia saved my sanity," I said. "Laura announced that she was tired of dormitory life, and with her trust fund she could easily afford to rent half the house from me. She moved in and we scrubbed and painted and redecorated until it didn't feel like the same place any more. And Aunt Georgia made me buy ammunition for my father's old gun and take the gun safety and target shooting courses and get a gun safe and a concealed carry license."

"You couldn't report the attack? Oh, no, of course not. Too bad nobody told you not to destroy the evidence."

My cheeks flamed. "Report what? A drunken hookup that I subsequently regretted? No crime there. And I didn't want to tell anybody what an *idiot* I'd been. Anyway, he didn't hurt me."

"We see that differently. But as for the idiocy factor... Oh, well, as one of our previous Presidents said, 'When I was young and stupid, I was young and stupid.' Some day remind me to tell you some of the stupid stunts *I* pulled when I was nineteen."

"Oh?" I perked up slightly at the promise of hearing about somebody else's dumb mistakes. "Like what?"

"Well, there was the thing about practicing five-point landings off the bar..." He saw my puzzled look and started over. "Parachute school. You're supposed to land on the balls of your feet, fall back onto the side of your calf, side of your thigh – keep rolling – hip, back. Then roll back forwards into a standing position."

I tried to picture it. "Wouldn't it be simpler not to fall over in the first place?"

"Absolutely, if your parachute cooperates. If anything goes wrong, well, this is supposed to be the best way of avoiding injury from hitting the ground at high speed. And we tested it thoroughly."

"Off the bar?"

"Evenings, after classes. One thing we did learn right away, it's best to clear away any glassware that might get knocked onto the floor before you start to 'practice.'" He opened his left hand to display a curving dark-red line crossing his palm. "A second thing I learned at approximately the same time: there are a *lot* of nerve endings in the palm of your hand. So where do we stand in the Stupid Sweepstakes?"

I laughed. Still a little shaky. "I don't know. How are we scoring it?"

"My personal theory is, anybody who survived being nineteen gets extra credit. So we're both pretty well off on points. And now..." He stretched. I couldn't help but notice how the movement strained the shirt over his chest and shoulders. Not that this had relevance to anything. "Now I'd better get on with that laundry. No, don't get up. I am going to impress you with my domestic competence."

The pile of sheets, bedding and dirty clothes he carried through the kitchen a few minutes later was certainly damp enough, but it didn't seem to reek as badly as I'd feared.

"It's bad enough," he said, wrinkling his nose after he dumped everything into the washer on the back porch, "but I'm counting on the miracle of modern detergents to neutralize it. I certainly don't want Cathlugs thinking he's just christened himself a new latrine on my bed."

"Cath Palug."

"Whatever. Why don't you get him fixed?"

"You must not have looked closely. He *is* fixed. But he didn't move in with us until a couple of years ago – that's when we took him to the vet – and I think by then it was too late in some ways. His self-image was already set."

"Oh well, as long as he doesn't push me into a bog and take my car keys – that's as close to a kingdom as I've got, that vintage Mustang outside that I restored myself – I figure I'm ahead of the game."

I liked the way his voice softened when he referred to his car.

I liked even more the evidence that he'd actually listened when I told him the legend that inspired Cath Palug's naming, even if he did have a bit of trouble getting the name right.

And the way his shirt strained across his chest when he stretched... well, that was something a sensible landlady with a realtor's license and a handful of language students would not think about, not in connection with a man who'd blown into my life without warning and would probably blow out the same way, any day now.

He had never even told me what he was doing here in Austin. If he lived here already, why was he renting a room from me? And if he didn't, how did he know where to find an indoor shooting range and a dark sports bar?

Too many questions surrounded that man, and for once I couldn't convince myself that it was too much trouble to look for the answers.

13. Right angles and cutting corners

But I didn't have the energy to interrogate Michael right then. I wanted a break. I wanted to stop worrying about people and about the past and go into a world where I felt fully competent and never made stupid mistakes.

Language.

It had been my salvation innumerable times. Learning Farsi, for instance, had actually been a secondary effect of that mess in my sophomore year; I decided to learn a new language to keep my mind occupied. Since I'd already invested the effort in learning the Arabic alphabet, another but unrelated language that used the same script seemed like a good choice; my talent for spoken language doesn't extend to reading strange alphabets, which is as much work for me as for anyone else. It was way too late in the semester to sign up for the Farsi class, and anyway I needed to work faster than the regular class schedule if I was to crowd other thoughts out of my mind. I arranged a tutoring swap: Nilufer, a graduate student born in Iran, taught me Farsi and in return I taught her how to write papers in academic-ese (a deservedly unpopular dialect of English).

I didn't have an informant for a new language handy right now, but I had the next best thing hidden between the mattress and box spring in my bedroom. I told Michael I was meeting friends for dinner, shut myself in the bedroom to change into something appropriately dressy, slipped the notebook into my tote bag and took off down the street at a brisk walk.

It took half an hour to walk to the office, and I needed the time to clear my head. I was relieved to find the house empty; Aunt Georgia must be out on an actual date. I stifled a slight pang of envy with the reminder that I didn't need the expected lecture from Aunt Georgia about socializing with my colleagues. With the place to myself I quietly let myself into my aunt's office, commandeered the extremely powerful reading lamp she'd invested in to put off the day of requiring glasses, and opened up the notebook for a few hours of quiet study and record-keeping.

This was the first chance I'd had to look over the material in peace and quiet since the night before Michael and I went into the shooting range, and I had just read through it then without making a proper systematic analysis of the data. Now, as I grew absorbed in the task, the world around me faded into insignificance. Nothing was real except the circle of bright lamplight and the wavering German script scribbled across the tall, narrow pages. Whoever made the notes had obviously been attempting to collect the standard forms that should have supported a transformational grammar of the language when he had enough data. But he'd also, equally obviously, had some trouble doing that. A few German sentences scribbled at the bottom of one page complained that his informants were deliberately misunderstanding him. Pages of random vocabulary interspersed with a very few sentence forms suggested that either the complaint was accurate, or that the writer wasn't very good at field work.

I withheld judgment.

Tonight, in this office, I was enjoying a privilege the compiler of this notebook might never have had: the chance to look over all the data in peace, collating similar phrases and sentences from the entire notebook and sketching out the underlying design of the language.

It was this overall view that helped me see what the original researcher seemed to have missed: the most common sentence forms, the ones he took to be the basic structures of the language, were significantly more complicated than the rare short sentences jotted down here and there.

That is something that just doesn't happen in any language I've studied. Think about it. "Sam went to the game." Five words. "Sam might possibly have gone to the game at some time." Eleven words.

Human beings: we're hard-wired to save ourselves effort. Look at the neat sidewalks on a university campus, meeting at right angles and delineating squares and rectangles of grass; then look at the diagonal paths traced by generations of students cutting across the grass. No, it's not original sin; it's something that probably got built into us in hunter-gatherer days. Calories were scarce, and the tribe members who burned fewer calories by taking the most efficient path had a slight reproductive advantage that got amplified by generations upon generations of selection.

The same sort of thing is true of language. In most languages, the simplest forms go with the simplest and most common statements. Past, present, future indicative verbs are pretty straightforward. Get into the subjunctive, talking about what might be instead of what is, and life immediately gets more complicated. It's not literally a matter of counting words, but in general the plain indicative statement will be shorter and simpler than its subjunctive counterpart.

I was willing to bet fifty bucks and my linguistics degree that whoever compiled this notebook had made a mistake so serious that it almost had to have been the result of a deliberate deception. And I mentally apologized to the author for surmising that he was inept at field work. He had been quite right: for whatever reason, his informants had been misleading him. And it mattered – it made all the difference in the world!

The annotations showed that they had told him that "Djnd vla!!mqd bze dzlaamk," meant "The wool is clean," and "Djnd vlaad dzlaamk," meant "The wool might become clean some time." That "Dzhla#m qto!!mqd bze ghri," meant "The projectile moves straight," and that "Q!x qto! ghri," meant "The girl might be walking straight."

Like I said – it's not as simple as counting words or syllables – but languages just don't like to work that way. People who really talked as the informants claimed would…. Would probably walk in straight lines and take right-angle turns to navigate around a trackless highland valley. I didn't believe it for a minute. The researcher who compiled this notebook must have been so focused on collecting his samples that he'd overlooked huge, gaping inconsistencies between what he'd been told and the way people actually use language.

Okay, if you're not asleep by now, you're probably fidgeting in your seat and muttering, "Who cares about the difference between one verb form and another? Why should *I* care?"

Well – I don't know about you, but *I* cared because by this time, I had also figured out why saying some things in what this researcher called Alt-Shaimaki changed the universe, while other statements were magically inert. Yes, I'm calling it magic. You think of a term you like better, feel free to use it. When *I* can make clients happy with a house they'd been about to reject, or create a picture-perfect tight grouping of shots after not practicing at the range for years, just by saying something under my breath, I call that magic. You call it what you like.

By now I wasn't working just on the memory of those two episodes, you see. The vocabulary and phrases I'd been analyzing had given me plenty of material for experiments. In fact, it had been a very productive evening. I now had:

1. A working theory of how the magic in this language worked. To talk about things without altering the state of the universe, you used the subjunctive; to make things actually happen, you used the indicative. The informants had probably switched their translations around to make it harder for outsiders to work this out – maybe even hoping that their seeming cooperation would discourage the researcher and send him away. Unfortunately, they hadn't been totally consistent with this tactic, and the few phrases that did work would have encouraged him to keep prying until...

2. Until what? Well, the evening's study had also shown me that the bigger the change, the bigger the headache. Making a pencil disappear cost me a single stab of pain; making Aunt Georgia's antique French clock vanish into thin air had given me a nasty migraine that still hadn't gone away. (Not to mention the headache of replacing that clock. I should have practiced on something less valuable.) Given the increased trouble I was having concentrating, I feared that I'd done myself more damage than just a temporary headache. If the original researcher had been incautious, might he

have killed himself by overuse of the language? Problem, from the point of view of the native informants, solved – or it would have been, if Koshan Idrisov hadn't stolen the notebook and tried to sell it. They must not have known about that notebook. Hmm, and did something about the language explain what had happened to Koshan? Had he made himself disappear by accident? What happened if you said "M?n vlaad kzmtq," or "I am nowhere?" I decided not to test that query.

3. I also had the data from the notebook stored as a series of images. I'd photographed the pages with my cell phone, sent them to my office computer, and downloaded them to the spare flash drive I kept in my top desk drawer. Now I could give Dr. Osborne the notebook, get him out of my hair, and continue studying the language at my leisure… if I dared. I would think about that tomorrow, when my headache would have abated and I could think straight again.

I tore my notes into minuscule scraps and dropped them in the wastepaper basket before leaving the office. My headache let up slightly on the walk home; darkness and fresh air both helped, giving me the hope that I hadn't inflicted permanent damage on myself while experimenting with Alt-Shaimaki. The only problem was the occasional car flashing its headlights into my eyes. That hurt enough that I took to standing still, staring away from the street, every time I heard a car engine.

Except for a light in Michael's room, the house was dark. Laura was probably still out singing at the White Horse. I didn't need to deal with Michael again tonight, so I decided to try and get inside without his noticing me. I wanted to talk to Laura first, to tell her what I'd figured out about Alt-Shaimaki. Maybe by the time she got up tomorrow I would have recovered enough to give her a small – a *very* small – demonstration. Maybe I could "disappear" a dust bunny or the tip of a pencil. A whole pencil? That might be pushing it.

I let myself into the house quietly, didn't turn on any lights, and – in comfortable darkness – put the notebook away in my gun safe where I should have been keeping it all along. Good, this time I remembered. I hoped that was a sign that any brain damage caused by the language repaired itself with a little rest. It wasn't like I could exactly ask a neurologist about that.

I let myself into the bathroom and felt in the medicine cabinet without turning on any lights. There should be a bottle of aspirin… Okay. Good. I shook a tablet into my hand, tasted it to make sure it was the aspirin and not some other small pill, shook out two more and felt for the plastic glass to get some water.

A voice from Michael's room froze me where I stood, hand on the faucet.

***

After Sienna went out, Michael had tried to watch a movie in the living room. Couldn't keep his mind on it. He locked up the house and went for a long walk; that didn't work either. Finally, back in his rented room, he called Hank.

"I have the data," he said as soon as his employer answered. "I can fly out tomorrow to bring it to you."

"You've got the notebook? Good man!"

It would be easy to let that statement pass, but for some reason he couldn't do it. "I've got all the information that was in the notebook. That's what you wanted, isn't it?"

"I want the *notebook*," Hank said testily. "You know that. I can't risk letting Ed Osborne or anybody else getting hold of it."

"Why? Are you afraid he'll publish before you?"

"If what I suspect is true, it'll be a disaster if *anybody* publishes that information. You have to get the notebook away from her."

"I'm not going to steal from her."

"Interesting moral stance. You don't mind stealing the *information*, but you draw the line at the book? You're not against stealing, Ryan, you're just against getting caught."

So much for compromising with his conscience.

"She's a good person, and she's had too much to deal with already. I'm sorry, Hank. You need to go pick on somebody your own size. I'm not going to help you persecute this woman just to get you another exotic curio."

Hank spoke, agitatedly, loudly, and at some length. Michael held the phone away from his ear as his employer's voice rose. His own eyebrows rose as he took in what the man was saying.

"Excuse me, you *believe* this? You think people can do magic just by chanting the right mystical phrases from some obscure language?"

"There's no chanting and no mysticism involved, Ryan," Hank snapped. "There have been weird stories about the Shaimaki for years, and the man who brought that notebook to this country showed me enough to corroborate those stories. Call it magic, call it a little-known side effect of quantum physics if it makes you happier, but he demonstrated the language to me. I'm not just looking for another item for my collection this time. I'm trying to save the world."

"Isn't that a bit of hyperbole, even for you? How do you think some illegible scribbles in a grease-stained notebook are going to destroy the world?"

"Ask the men who worked on the Manhattan Project," Hank snapped.

"A bit late for that... I'm sorry, Hank. I can't believe you, and I'm not going to lie and steal for you this time. You don't have to pay me... although I *did* get you the information you said you wanted."

"I'll pay you triple rates if you get that notebook away from her! Don't you see, Ryan, *she can read it!* That makes her as dangerous as Osborne!"

Michael sighed. If he closed his eyes, he could see the jagged script and jumble of symbols that filled the pages he'd photographed. "How do you know she can read it? I sure as hell couldn't make head nor tail out of the thing."

"You're not my only source of information," Hank told him.

"Oh? Who else have you paid to spy on her for this famous notebook? Besides me, I mean."

Before Hank could reply he heard the bathroom door open and whirled to see Sienna standing there in the peasant blouse and full crinkly skirt she'd donned for her dinner date.

She was white as a ghost again, freckles standing out across her nose, lipstick a glaring contrast to her skin tones. How much had she heard?

"It was all about the notebook, then?"

Her husky half-whisper broke his heart.

"You were spying on me all along. I suppose Dr. Osborne sent you. Just like he sent Paco, and the jerk who tried to rent the room before you and then broke into the house. I should have realized you were just another one of his flunkies."

"Sienna, no! I'm not…"

She cut him off with a wave of her hand. "Why should I believe anything you say? I've heard enough. I want you out of this house by morning."

"I have a lease," Michael said.

He realized a moment later that that hadn't just been the wrong thing to say; it had been an *extremely* wrong thing to say.

"If you have any sense of decency – which I doubt – you'll tear up that lease and get out of here tomorrow. Oh, don't worry. I'll refund your money. That's what it's all about for you, isn't it? Money."

14. Never show an open house by yourself

I was scheduled to show an open house with Davis the next morning. I would have preferred something that would keep me too busy to think – open houses often involved long spells of boredom punctuated by rushes of several potential clients at once – but at least this allowed me to be out of my own house for the day. With any luck, by the time I returned Michael would have moved out.

That prospect didn't actually make me feel any happier, no matter how many times I told myself that all I wanted was to be let alone to live what had been a perfectly acceptable, if not exactly thrilling, life before magical languages and burglarizing thugs had turned everything upside down.

Probably I was too worried about the dangerous possibilities of Alt-Shaimaki to feel good about anything until I'd puzzled out what to do with my new understanding. Now that I had thought about it, I'd realized that I could no longer hand over the notebook to Dr. Osborne and bow out of the loop. In the last few days he'd revealed himself to be unscrupulous and slightly unbalanced – not that unusual, really, for a tenured professor. A lot of them had left the wreckage of other people's careers behind in their scramble to reach the top; I knew that, and if I'd stayed in academia I wouldn't have turned my back on most of my colleagues. But in Dr. Osborne's case it was worse. Not only would I not have trusted him with my career (if I'd had one); I dared not trust him with the level of power Alt-Shaimaki offered.

I wasn't sure I trusted myself with it, but at least I had a healthy respect for the dangers of overusing the language.

I tried to imagine who could be trusted with this kind of information. Somebody strong-minded, steady, reliable…

Couldn't picture it. An image of Michael Ryan kept coming into my head. Probably because he'd proved himself to be the exact opposite of all that.

By the time I reached the house we were supposed to be showing, I was in a flaming temper and had a raging headache without even using a single word of Alt-Shaimaki. I was early; Davis hadn't shown up yet, and the family who lived there were hustling through an early breakfast before decamping for the day. Mrs. Rivers was kind enough to offer me a cup of coffee while she washed up the breakfast dishes and shoved them into the dishwasher.

"If anybody wants to see how the dishwasher works, the detergent pods are in this canister," she told me.

"You don't mind if I run it?"

"My dear, I'd be delighted!" Mrs. Rivers ran fingers through her short curls, turned to shout, "Billy, put those running shoes in the closet or I'm donating them to Goodwill!" at a teenage boy, and tried to refill my brimming coffee mug for the third time. "Do you take milk? Oh, sorry, I already asked that. Jessie May Rivers, quit fooling with your phone and get ready to go! Ms. Brown, feel free to make yourself more coffee, just be sure and put your mug in the dishwasher when you're done, okay?"

"It's driving me crazy," she confided while the two kids clumped up and down the stairs, "trying to live here while keeping most of our possessions out of sight and maintaining perfect cleanliness just in case somebody wants to see the house. I do nothing but run the dishwasher and do the laundry and yell at the kids to pick up their stuff. Today will be like a vacation. George and I are going to take the kids to Schlitterbahn, and I won't have to clean up after them for the whole day! Do you think this open house will work?"

From her point of view, that meant, "Will anybody make an offer?" I decided it would be needlessly unkind to tell her that from a realtor's point of view, the reason for spending all day guarding an open house was not so much to sell the place, as to collect names and addresses of potential clients who might wander in. "You never know," I said vaguely, and decided to run the dishwasher and put up the clean dishes regardless of whether anybody wanted an appliance demonstration. The woman clearly needed a break.

They left barely ahead of the scheduled opening time, and I was too busy for the next few minutes to call Davis and ask what was keeping him. There were throw pillows on the living room floor to pick up and various bits of flotsam from the Rivers' daily lives to hide in a closet. Even after cleaning up the obvious things, I kept finding junk strewn around by the kids that also had to be hidden in order to give the house that "newly decorated, never really lived in," look that was *de rigueur* for showings. By the time I was ready to set up my brochures and visitors' book on the dining room table, I had a new appreciation for Mrs. Rivers' problems. Maybe she could board the two teenagers somewhere else while they were trying to sell the house? Like, the nearest kennel?

The doorbell rang and I hustled to meet the first viewers, pasting a welcoming smile on my face. It was *good* that there were people so eager that they showed up the minute the open house was supposed to start. Wasn't it?

Half an hour later, after three separate couples had tramped through the house – none of whom had been willing to fork over their names and addresses for my visitors' book a.k.a. potential clients list – I found out why we were drawing such a crowd.

"Oh, you don't need our address, we're not looking to buy," the last woman confided in me. "And we live just down the street. We just wanted to see what Sophie Rivers has done with the place. For the last year she's been telling everybody how much they've spent on remodeling and decorators, trying to turn this house into her dream home. But she never invited anybody over! And now George has been transferred and they have to sell. Karma, I call it." She sniffed disdainfully at the black tiles and granite-topped counters in the kitchen. "Very trendy, I suppose, but I prefer something a little more traditional. *We* have lived here since 1978 and never felt the need to tear out and replace the center of our home."

I had a mental picture of her kitchen: avocado tiles and dusty yellow appliances.

"Is everybody who's come in a neighbor?" The two preceding couples were still poking around, making jokes about the jacuzzi in the master bathroom.

The woman I was talking to sniffed again. "Naturally. *Everybody* was curious."

If so, then the block must be underpopulated; after that early whirlwind of activity, nobody at all turned up for quite a while. I had plenty of time to stare at my disgracefully pristine visitors' book. And to call Davis.

I could tell from his voice when he answered that I wasn't going to have a partner today. "Davis, you sound terrible. Allergies?"

"I wish," he said, or rather croaked. "But it feels bore like flu. I told Georgia I wouldd't be id. I'b sorry, Siedda. I guess I could cobe over..."

"No, thanks, I don't need you sharing whatever bug you've got with me – not to mention the rest of the neighborhood, who have been trooping in for a free look at the Rivers' remodeling job."

"I dod't like you beidg there alode. You could call Carly."

"She's got other things to do. Don't worry, Davis, I can handle it. It's not like we're exactly being swarmed by potential clients. So far, we're just providing free entertainment for the neighbors." I had no idea what Carly's schedule was, but I would take the "risk" of running an open house by myself over the certainty of hearing her embellishment on the terrible experience she hadn't really had once.

In the next three hours I had just two more visitors, a young couple who brightly admitted they weren't really in the market for anything more pricey than a condo in Round Rock. They had just decided to drop in and look at a really nice house to cheer themselves up.

I didn't even try very hard to get them to sign the visitors' book, but they did anyway. Oh well, maybe seeing one signature would inspire others to follow suit.

Two or three apparent signups would be even better, wouldn't they?

My tote bag yielded two different ballpoint pens and an ultra-fine black Sharpie. I added Rebecca Sharp of Vanity Place, J. Kilroy@was_here.com, and Mme. Defarge of Rue Robespierre, Paris to the single kosher entry in the visitors' book, making a mental note to warn Aunt Georgia not to bother with the first four names. I was modestly proud of Mme. Defarge, who had signed up in a sophisticated, spiky handwriting not dissimilar to German script and quite different from the clunky, graffiti-like capitals of J. Kilroy. Maybe I could add document forgery to my modest skill set? Michael would probably know whether there was much of a demand for people to fake doctors' notices and accountants' letters...

Not that I would be asking the rat, even in the very unlikely event that I ever saw him again.

I played with my phone again, looking at the photos I'd snapped the night before. I wouldn't have minded if they were a little bit higher-resolution; when I blew them up enough to read individual words, the slashing black lines of German script were just a bit fuzzy. Still legible, though.

Still tempting. Still dangerous.

If I'd found a sentence that meant, "Many people want to buy the house," I would have been sorely tempted. Wait, I could almost construct that; this was the word for "many," and "people" occurred on the second page of the notebook – a quick search for that picture – and –

And I needed to stop scrolling through these photos before I put together something I might carelessly subvocalize. I wasn't crazy enough to risk brain damage just to score points in the real estate game! A good thing I'd left the actual notebook locked in my gun safe...

Bet you Michael can pick that lock.

"It's a combination lock," I told the irritating voice in my head.

All the same.

"Well, I hope he does! Then it'll go away, and he'll go away, and my life can go back to normal!"

Which was what I wanted. Really. Even if a return to the status quo did, just at that moment, seem depressingly bleak.

I stared into my phone screen and slowly scrolled through the picture of that second page of the notebook. The phrase "The kindling burns" caught my eye. The translation was wrong; I now knew that the sentence meant, "The kindling might burn." But it was easy enough to strip out the subjunctive markers for a sentence that would act upon reality. If I could find a word for "notebook" I could substitute it for "kindling" and turn the damned thing to ash. Yeah, well, not a good idea. If it was still in the gun safe with my loaded gun... I really had no idea what would happen. Maybe there wouldn't be enough oxygen for a fire. Maybe the gun would explode. Maybe the language wouldn't know which notebook I meant, since I wasn't looking directly at it, and would do something haywire like setting all the notebooks in a two-block radius on fire. *Ten*-block radius. It would take a lot of experimentation to calibrate the effect of different phrases. Even if I figured that something like twenty-four hours between uses would allow my brain to recover from each use – and it might be forty-eight hours, or six weeks or worse for all I knew – I'd be in a nursing home before I'd tested everything properly.

Or maybe Michael had already broken into the gun safe, and had that notebook in his hands right now, and wouldn't it serve him right if it burst into flames? Now *that* would be a temptation worth succumbing to… but again, I'd need to be looking directly at the thing. Both for accuracy, and so I could enjoy the moment.

I was relishing that fantasy, and staring into my phone, when a footstep behind me startled me. I sat up with a start… and possibly saved my life, because the blow that fell partly on the chair and partly on my shoulder would have hit my head otherwise.

I wasn't thinking about that right then, though. There was this amazing pain in my shoulder, and a moment later the chair was jerked out from under me and I hit the carpet so hard that the pain flared up to nova level, and then I did black out.

When I came to, my shoulder hurt even more, and it had been wrenched into an agonizing position behind my back. Both my arms were pulled back, and there was something wrapped around my wrists that kept them there. My head had to be on the floor, didn't it, because all I could see was carpet and the table legs. I moaned and the toe of a polished shoe moved into my line of vision.

"I told you this was not over," said Edward Osborne's hateful, precise, gloating voice above me. "*Where is it?*"

I rolled onto my side and craned my head so I could see him. "Not here."

"I know that." He gestured beyond the table, and I saw the contents of my tote bag spilled out onto the carpet. My phone was underneath everything else. Good. It hadn't occurred to him to look at the phone. Well, it wouldn't would it? He was an old guy, he probably thought a phone was something black that hung on the wall. He certainly wouldn't think of a phone the way my generation did, as a repository for data and photos and all the details of your life.

"You are going to take me to your house and give me the notebook."

"That won't work. I mean, the bank is closed by now." It had to be after two.

He shook his head and gave me a thin-lipped, terrifying smile. He reminded me of Frau Heilemann when she was about to tell some poor terrified student exactly how badly he'd done on the mid-term exam. Or of himself nine years ago, for that matter, castigating the entire class and recommending that we switch majors to Education or Music Therapy or something equally undemanding. Some people really enjoy delivering bad news.

"I hope for your sake that it is not in a bank vault."

"Why?" The damn thing *should* be in a bank vault. If I'd thought of that in time, it would be.

"Because I propose to hurt you until you are more than eager to hand it over."

I'd been way too casual about this notebook. Of course, I hadn't realized just how dangerous it could be until last night. And then other things had driven it out of my mind. Little things like lies, and betrayal, and that sense of the floor falling out from under you when you discover that once again you've trusted the last person you should ever have believed in.

Michael.

The sense of loss was so strong that I actually hallucinated: thought I saw his face at the window beyond Dr. Osborne. I blinked away tears.

"The OPEN HOUSE sign has been removed," he told me, still with that chilly smile on his face, "and the doors are locked. We will not be disturbed."

"Good luck with that," I said, "all the neighbors were dying to see the results of the redecoration. They mobbed this place all morning and there are still dozens of people who haven't been by yet. They'll be pounding on the door."

He picked up the visitors' book and showed me the open page – blank but for the one sign-up and my three forgeries. "I don't think so. If you had only four callers up to now, the interest in this place is not that great."

"And the family will be back soon."

"Oh? How strange, given that the open house was to continue until six o'clock. You do not make up very plausible lies." He stepped back, out of my vision, and I heard paper rustling. "Just let me know when you are ready to give up the notebook." The paper rustled again and he said, slowly and carefully, "*Q!x ynd?mqd bze moq.*"

Subjunctive. He'd just said, "The girl *might* burn." Naturally, nothing happened. I forced a laugh. "You don't understand the language, do you?"

"It should work! This page—"

If he was working off a copy of just one page, he didn't have enough context to figure things out as I'd done.

"You idiot," I said. It was marvelously refreshing to say that to a full professor. And how convenient that his reference was a verb I'd just been thinking about! "Your accent sucks, and what's more you got it wrong! Let me help you out. *O!dm ynd?moq.*" *The man burns.*

Shadows swept down on the room, and I felt my body being tugged sideways, then up. My head started hurting. But it worked: flames crackled and Osborne screamed. I heard him dancing up and down, and then he kicked me in the ribs. "Make it stop! Stop it!"

I didn't quite know how to do that. What was the word for 'not?' I could hardly look it up on my phone while I was tied up.

He dodged and danced around the room, beating at the flames, then threw himself down on the rug and rolled, trying to put them out.

"*O!dm ynd?moq,*" I chanted. My head was killing me, but I didn't dare let up for fear he'd attack me again. I was so dizzy I might have been spinning in mid-air, and the shadowy room was bright with pinpricks of light like distant stars, and I couldn't pause to think about any of it. "*O!dm ynd?moq, O!dm ynd?moq, O!dm...*" Damn! I couldn't remember the rest of the sentence.

When I shut up, I could hear other sounds: Osborne's screams, and glass breaking.

Glass breaking?

A man came through the window, pushing the frame out of shape and cursing under his breath. He grabbed a throw off the living room couch and wrapped it around Osborne, stifling the flames. Then he knelt by me and sliced through the tape on my wrists.

"Saving your employer?" I flexed my aching arms and sat up, looking from Michael to Osborne and back. "Why didn't you just help him torture me?"

"He's not my employer," Michael said between his teeth, "and I'm saving *you*." He turned his head and snapped, "Stop that!" Osborne was whining in pain.

Using that language had given me the usual headache, this time with a side of dizziness. Still sitting on the carpet, I said, "Whose side are you on, anyway?"

"Not his."

"How many sides are there?"

"You'd be surprised."

I gave up. "My phone is under that little heap of stuff over there. Can I have it?"

"What for?"

"To call the police, obviously."

Osborne stopped whining and grated out, "*M?n vlaad udjy.*"

And the throw that had been wrapped around him slowly subsided onto the carpet, empty.

What had he said? 'I become... *udjy*.' I couldn't remember what *udjy* meant. A place? Somewhere else, presumably.

Michael looked as white as he had on the night we met, even though this time nobody was pointing a gun at him. He kept looking at the patch of carpet where Osborne had been rolling, then at me, then back at the empty blanket on the carpet. He stepped over and prodded it with his toe. "My God," he breathed, "Hank was telling the truth!"

"And you're in shock because you never tell the truth yourself, so you don't expect it of anybody else!" I levered myself back up to the chair and shaded my eyes with one hand. "Who's Hank?"

"Where did he go?"

"Who, Hank?"

"The *professor*."

"I don't know." I glanced up at him. "And that also is the truth. I'm just explaining because you may not recognize it. Given your style."

Michael sighed, rubbed his eyes, looked again at the folds of the blanket. "Okay. I'm not working with that guy, but I admit that I didn't tell you everything. Are you going to hate me forever?"

"Why shouldn't I?"

"Well, I did just save your life."

"I was saving my own life just fine," I snapped. "I set Osborne on fire, and he made himself vanish. Your participation was minimal at best."

"Oh, well, excuse me for interfering! Want me to duct tape your wrists together again so you can continue from where I so rudely interrupted?"

I put a hand over my eyes. The headache was so fierce that I was leaking tears. "I want…"

But whatever I'd been going to say disappeared into the colorless, formless fluff that was filling my head. When I tried to remember what had just happened, the pain jolted through my forehead again.

"I need to talk to Laura," I mumbled.

15. This thing burns

It was getting dark outside when I woke up to Cath Palug's affectionate kneading and purring. The kneading involved claws. Affectionately, of course. I was in my room, and somebody was sitting in the rocking chair.

"Feeling better?" Laura asked. As my eyes adjusted to the dimness, I saw that she was dressed up as if she were about to go out. That cold-shoulder red dress of hers, the one with the sequins and the tight waist, would have been only marginally legal for normal street wear.

I moved my head cautiously. "Yes. Why aren't you singing somewhere?"

"I do occasionally have a night off, you know."

"A *Saturday* night?"

She sighed. "Paco's drummer got arrested, he couldn't find a stand-in, Harry at the White Horse said he's never booking us to open on a weekend again."

"Oh." After waiting a moment to see if the needles of pain were going to start up again, I added, "I'm sorry." The only needles I felt were those Cath Palug was lovingly implanting in my back.

She waved her hand. "Easy come, easy go. You planning to tell me how your fun-filled Saturday went?"

Osborne screaming as the flames licked him. "I'm not sure I can remember all of it." What had happened after that?

"Mike brought you home."

"Mike?"

"*Michael Ryan*," she said impatiently. "Come on, I know it's a common

117

name, but how many Mikes are in your life right now?"

"Well, not him. I hate him." Unlike my memories of this afternoon, the memory of last night, my discovery of what a two-timing double-dealing bastard he was, was still crystal clear. "Wait, does he still have a key? I told him to get out."

"He brought you home, and you have a key to your own house," Laura said. "He called me and said somebody needed to sit with you, you were confused and incoherent. But by the time I got here you were asleep."

"Oh… Laura. You didn't cancel a *gig* to sit here with me, did you?"

"No, I told you what happened."

"But that dress…"

"I canceled a date," she told me. "Duke – you know, Paco's lead guitarist – and I were going to go out and drown our sorrows. Listen to a bunch of other bands and badmouth them, you know? Nothing that can't wait. Why do you suddenly hate Mike?"

I told her how I'd overheard him last night, as good as admitting that someone had paid him to spy on me because of that blasted notebook – "You know, the one with the language that you think doesn't do magic? Laura, it *does*. I figured it all out last night." That study session in my aunt's office was much clearer to me than today's events. "It's a good thing that notebook only holds a small vocabulary and a few examples of sentences, because someone with a complete mastery of the language could… could probably conquer the world," I said, with a chill going through me as I voiced what I'd been trying not to think.

"*Uh*-huh," Laura said, with a heavy layer of sarcasm. "Tell me again about the people who speak this language?"

"I don't know much," I admitted. "They live somewhere in the Pamirs, in one of the high-altitude valleys that gets cut off from the world a lot, which may explain why the language hasn't totally died out. I can deduce something about their way of life from the examples in the notebook. They care a lot about different grades of wool, they grow and harvest wheat, they have fruit trees and dry the fruit to help get them through the winter. They use sheep for wool and meat, yaks for transport, spread the dung on their fields and dry it for fuel, make butter from the milk and put it in their tea. That's pretty standard, I think, in that harsh climate; people need the fat and calories in the butter."

"I see," Laura said with her three-cornered grin. "Sounds like a hand-to-mouth existence. Lots of hard work and not many comforts."

"Life in the High Pamirs is hard," I said.

"So… if these guys speak a language that they can use to conquer the world, why are they living at the ends of the earth and trying to scrape a living out of some high-altitude valleys? Why are they burning yak shit and drinking butter tea? Why haven't they used these great powers of theirs to get, I don't know, central heating and grocery delivery? This doesn't make any sense, Sienna. Just like all fantasies about magic, it falls apart when you look at the details. That's what's wrong with so many fantasy novels," she went on, "too many of the writers don't bother to design a plausible society and they have no clue how an economy works, so they can't answer questions like that. I understand this is your first attempt at fantasy—"

"Laura. *This is not a fantasy.* Okay, I don't have all the answers yet. But I do have some theories. For starters, using the language to change the universe costs the user something. I've only done a few little things, but every single time I've paid with a bad headache. And the more I do, the more confused I get and the worse my memory is. If one of the Shaimaki tried to use the language to conquer the world, he'd probably kill himself before he got close."

"Using this language gives you a headache? So? Trying to speak Spanish gives me a headache! What do you call it, anyway? I can't go on saying 'this language.'"

"Why not?" I thought back to the pages I'd studied last night. "Whoever collected the information in the notebook called it Alt-Shaimaki. In English, that would be Old Shaimaki. The people who speak it – the ones the writer studied, anyway – must live around Lake Shaimak."

"And where's that when it's at home?"

I waved my hand. "Somewhere in Central Asia. The guy Thalia sent to rent a room from me, the one who brought the notebook with him, he was from Taklanistan. From the Pamirs. So… was he one of the native speakers the writer studied? But then why would he need the notebook? There's a lot I haven't figured out yet."

"Including why these uniquely powerful people spend their lives herding yaks and drinking tea with butter in it."

"No, I told you. There's a price to pay for using the language. Just making Aunt Georgia's antique wall clock disappear gave me a blinding migraine."

"You threw out your aunt's Art Deco clock? You're going to have a hell of a lot worse than a headache when she finds out!"

"I did not throw it out," I said. "I *made it disappear* without touching it. Granted, it wasn't the best choice for an experiment."

Laura snorted. "Sienna. Let's get back to reality. You cannot really make things disappear without touching them. Nobody can."

"Do you have a Kleenex?"

"No."

"A bobby pin?"

"I don't use them. Sienna, what is this about?"

"I'm not going to do anything big," I said, "but... oh, never mind. Just sit there and watch."

Standing up was tricky; I felt a little bit dizzy. But after swaying for a moment, I found my balance. I turned on the bedside lamp – I wasn't going to subject myself to the bright light of the ceiling fixture, even if the headache had receded – cleared a little space on top of my dresser and put an empty cough drop wrapper in the center of the space. "Watch this," I said, and pointed at the wrapper. "*Bu prdmt vlaad kzmtq!*" *This thing becomes nowhere.*

The ceiling fixture dimmed briefly as the wrapper disappeared. I rubbed my aching forehead.

Laura blinked and reached into the empty space where the wrapper had been.

"Nice trick!"

"Laura," I said desperately, "it's not a trick!" I was getting too upset to remember caution. "Watch this time, I'm going to set something on fire!" I scrabbled in the top drawer and pulled out an appointment card for my last visit to the dentist, eight months ago. "Hold this."

As soon as she took it between finger and thumb I pointed at the card and said, "*Bu prdmt ynd?moq!*" *This thing burns.*

I fought off a wave of giddiness; Laura screamed and dropped the flaming card on the rag rug. I hadn't thought through this very well, had I? I picked up a bedroom slipper, knelt to suffocate the tiny flame, and looked at the damage. In the soft light of the bedside lamp it didn't look that bad. I looked up at Laura.

She was dead white, all but her black hair and dark eyes.

"Sienna? That was real fire! It would have burned me! If th-that's a trick…"

"It isn't," I said, getting up slowly. "But I'm not going to do any more demos right now, if you don't mind." Lighting that card had brought back the ugly memories of this afternoon, now all too clear in my head. I kind of missed the white fuzz that had blurred them out for a while.

"I – I – That's okay. Yes." She took a deep breath and blew it out hard. "If this is for real, I don't need to see any more j-just now. And if it's a trick… Sienna, if you're teasing me, stop now, okay?"

"I'm not," I said. "It is real. This is why Dr. Edward Osborne was so desperate to get that notebook – and why he mustn't have it."

"What are we going to do?" Laura asked. "Burn it in front of him?"

"That would be a good idea. The trouble is, I don't exactly know where he is right now. He… kind of… went away this afternoon. Maybe he won't be back." I told Laura about the nasty scene at the Rivers open house. She listened without interrupting, still white-faced, twisting her hands together.

"Couldn't *you* make him go away? Permanently?"

I thought she hadn't fully grasped the situation. "Horrible things happen to people who overuse the language."

"Nothing horrible has happened to you. Yet. Well, except for what Dr. Osborne tried to do this afternoon, and you can't blame that on magic."

"That's because I haven't done very much. Only a couple of little nudges to the world. The worst thing was burning Dr. Osborne this afternoon."

"But you had to do that to save yourself!"

"I don't think the language cares about the purity of your motives," I said, thinking it out as I went. "I think it's more like gravity: if you jump off a cliff, you're going to fall, and gravity doesn't care that you had perfectly good reasons for jumping."

"Like to get away from the ax murderer who's chasing you."

"Exactly. And the higher the cliff, the worse the fall. You can still wind up dead at the bottom of the cliff, only from a broken neck instead of an ax in your head. I think it's like that. The bigger the change you make in the universe, the bigger the damage to your brain. If anybody did try to conquer the world, I think they'd become incurably mad before they got very far. Even if I did just a little more…"

"Like what?"

"If I could find the right words to use," I said slowly, "maybe I could make Michael tell me the truth."

"I thought you'd already decided that he was a liar and you hate him."

"I do!"

"But maybe you're hoping that there's a truth that exonerates him?"

"He did say that he's not working for Osborne." I thought it over. "And he didn't help Osborne."

"No. He got cut up and bruised coming in through a window to help *you*."

"He was hurt?"

"What, you didn't notice?"

"Everything was kind of fuzzy by then."

"Well, he stayed here – right by your side – until I got home. And he had blood on his shirt, not to mention a blood-stained handkerchief wrapped around one hand. Are you *sure* you hate him?"

I sighed. "I don't want to. But you didn't hear him last night… He's definitely been lying to me. He admitted as much today. Laura, I'm not terribly fond of guys who lie and trick their way into this house. And you have to admit I have a good reason for that."

"Maybe you should use the language to make him fall in love with you. Then he'd tell you the truth because he wants to."

"Or he'd come up with some other twisty reason that made it all right to lie… Anyway, I don't have the vocabulary for that either. The notebook is full of how to clean wool and dry yak dung patties. Not so much about feelings."

"Ah, so you have been thinking about it."

"No!"

"Well, you don't need to worry about the consequences of saying it, if you don't know what words to say. Maybe you should just try talking to him. You know. In English."

"I have nothing to say to that lying rat bastard."

"Well, maybe he has something to say to you."

It seemed to me that all Michael and I had to say to each other was 'Goodbye,' and that thought did not cheer me up. Wait, maybe I could make it stronger. "Come to think of it, I do want to say something to him."

"I knew it! What?"

"Don't let the door hit you on your way out."

16. Summer storm

Laura was inclined to drag out this useless conversation even farther, holding forth on the topic of stubborn grudge-holding women. After I refused to discuss Michael and convinced her that I really was okay, I managed to chase her out of the house to take up her interrupted not-really-a-date with Duke. The fact that she'd deployed that slinky red dress made me doubt her protestations that the "date" hadn't mattered to her, although I had better manners than to call her a liar to her face.

Once she was gone, I washed my face, made a cup of coffee and sat down to consider my problems. I needed to find Dr. Osborne and convince him the notebook was gone forever; burning it in front of him sounded like a great idea, but I hadn't yet figured out how to arrange it. Or where he was – I needed to find that word he'd used, *udjy*. Maybe it meant something like "in an alternate dimension inconsistent with human life," and that problem would be solved, yay.

Second, I needed to make sure Michael had moved out. I tiptoed through the bathroom and cracked the door into his bedroom. It wasn't bolted… but the bedroom was still full of his stuff. We would have to have another talk about that. If he thought saving my life made up for the previous lies… Huh. Should it? Well, I didn't need to think about that now; wherever the man might be, at least he wasn't here.

And third, I needed to confess to Aunt Georgia that the agency was on the hook for repairs to Sophie Rivers' front window. That, at least, I could tackle here and now. Bracing my shoulders, I reached for the phone.

"I know all about it," she interrupted before I got through my first sentence. "That nice young man you rented your front room to..."

I mentally substituted *That lying rat bastard I rented your front room to*, and missed the next few words. Police report. Insurance. Apologies to Rivers family. Everything was under control, my aunt said briskly, and all I needed to do was rest and feel better.

I guessed she hadn't missed her Art Deco clock yet. Or... had it magically popped back into existence? It wasn't like I'd done a lot of controlled research on what happened when you sent something into Nowhere. I decided not to raise the question; right now she wasn't mad at me, and it would be nice to have that last for a little while.

My head was better now, so after I got off the phone I skimmed through my images of the notebook, looking for the word Osborne had used. Ah, here it was: *udjy*, 'home.' Useful word. So he'd taken himself home, had he? I hoped doing so had given him a major headache on top of the pain from the burns. Now, would those have been real burns, or would he have been perfectly all right as soon as the magical flames were put out? I didn't feel like risking brain damage to research the question. On Monday I could call Sammy's big sister and find out if Osborne was in his office or in the hospital.

***

"Son," Hank Henderson said, "there's only one thing to do when a woman is this mad at you."

Michael had called Henderson to quit. When Hank asked why, he'd spilled out all the disasters of the last twenty-four hours. He had not asked for advice to the lovelorn.

"I have to be able to tell her that I'm not trying to steal her precious notebook. Not any longer."

"But you were," Hank pointed out, "and she's already plenty steamed about that." He paused. "Of course, since you're paying the price for that already, she probably wouldn't get much madder if you succeeded, so..."

"No."

"You want to walk away and leave her at the mercy of Ed Osborne? You think he's going to quit trying to get that notebook from whoever has it? Only way she'll be safe is when he knows for sure that somebody else has it. You'd be doing her a favor to steal it."

"No." After a wrenching evening of trying to persuade himself he hadn't seen anything unusual at that suburban open house, Michael had worked out his own solution. "The only way she – and the rest of the world – will be safe is if the notebook no longer exists, and Osborne knows *that* for sure."

A long silence. Finally Hank sighed. "You're probably right. Damn, I'd have liked to have that notebook. And *I* wouldn't have used it, you know. Heck, I can't even read that script. But it would be the only field notebook of Old Shaimaki in the world."

"A curio that's too expensive even for the Henderson fortune," Michael said. "Do you think any amount of money would stop Osborne from coming after it? And what if other people found out what the language can do?"

Hank sighed again. "Damn, I hate it when you're right. Okay… I'll pay you the same fee we agreed upon, if you can destroy the thing, document its destruction, and make sure Eddie Osborne understands that it's no longer available. And don't you dare tell anybody I'm going soft-headed in my old age, hear?"

Michael grinned. "I knew you'd do the right thing. Sir."

"Don't get too happy," Henderson warned him. "You've still got to persuade her to go along with you."

It was Michael's turn to sigh. "She hates me."

"Well, that gets us back to what I said: there's only one thing to do when a woman is this mad at you."

"Explain the situation?"

"Hell, no! Apologize! Grovel!"

"Apologize for what? I haven't done anything to her!"

"Except lie to her, search her room, photograph her notebook…"

"It's not really hers, and besides, she doesn't know about that part."

"Grovel," Hank repeated. "Then persuade her that it's got to be destroyed."

"What if I can't?"

"Then you'll have to do it in spite of her."

***

Going to sleep after all that wasn't really an option.

I stared up at the ceiling and counted the verb forms of Homeric Greek – there are around eight hundred of them, that alone usually put me to sleep before I got past the aorist subjunctive. Mentally reviewed my growing Old Shaimaki vocabulary. Recited the copious chunks of *Faust* that I had memorized in Frau Heilemann's high school German classes.

Nothing worked.

I decided that my fundamental mistake had been concentrating on Part I of Faust, which actually tells a story. Part II, which is full of arcane jibes at Goethe's literary contemporaries, would put anybody to sleep. But naturally, I hadn't memorized that part. At one time I would have said that was because learning Part II by heart could cause irreversible brain damage. Now that I had some experience of actual brain damage, that wasn't so funny. I just hoped it was reversible.

It was almost a relief when the downpour started. Rain drummed on the roof and thunder cracked overhead. For some time I tried to convince myself that all I heard was a late-summer storm rolling through town. But it didn't work; I kept hearing noises from the far side of the bathroom. Loud clunks and thuds sounded like somebody throwing the contents of the other bedroom against the wall. Either Michael was angry and packing up his possessions with maximum sound effects, or my wanna-be burglar had returned and was remarkably unconcerned about making enough noise to waken the residents – perhaps this time he was armed. In either case, I decided that I could use some extra security before checking out the noises.

"You don't need that," Michael said when I cracked the door from the bathroom into his bedroom. He nodded at my pistol. "I'm moving out. As you requested."

My knees were shaking for some reason. Had I really expected more of Osborne's thugs?

Well, why not?

I leaned against the doorjamb and slid down to sit on the floor, setting the Smith and Wesson down beside me. "I'm surprised."

"Why? You asked me to leave. I'm leaving."

I felt that as a conclusion, this left too much unsaid, but I didn't know where to start. "Do you customarily move after midnight?"

"I've been busy." He threw some clothes into a duffel bag and slammed the drawer he'd opened.

"Do you even have someplace to go?"

"Does it matter?"

It shouldn't. I reminded myself that I hated him. That he'd been lying to me from the beginning. That he'd inserted himself into *my house* with lies and secret motives.

"I… didn't mean to kick you out into the snow."

He laughed shortly. "In Austin? You'd have to wait a while and choose your time carefully. Don't worry. Kicking me out into the thunderstorm will have to do."

"You can stay until the rain stops."

"As long as you understand that I am effectively out of here."

"Why do you care?"

He slid down against the dresser to sit on the floor facing me. "Because I know how you feel about having your space invaded. Because I don't want you to associate me in any way with the jerk who assaulted you when you were nineteen. Because… I want you to listen when…" He exhaled a sharp breath and started over. "I want you to listen when I apologize."

"What exactly are you apologizing for?"

"Pretending I wasn't interested in the notebook, lying to you, taking money to spy on you. For starters. I need to *explain*…"

Until that moment, I hadn't realized that some idiotic part of me still hoped there was an explanation that would mean he hadn't been lying all along. I ran one finger along the barrel of the pistol. "I'm not sure the reasons make any difference."

"They have to!" he insisted. "You have to let me explain… Sure, I lied, but that's what – I mean, I didn't know it was *you* I was lying to."

I raised my brows. "Oh? Who did you think you were spying on?"

"Some woman. Koshan Idrisov's landlady. Could have been anybody. You see, I was in California when Hank contacted me. He told me there was a notebook he wanted… He's a collector. Exotic curios. He'd tried to negotiate with Idrisov to buy it but hadn't been able to get an answer. Initially he just wanted me to get in touch with Idrisov. Then I got out here and found out the guy had disappeared without packing up his stuff and nobody knew where he'd gone. I wanted to get a look at whatever he'd left…"

"Oh. Now we get to the part where you got paid to spy on me?"

"I didn't," Michael repeated, sounding strained, "know it was *you*."

"What's that supposed to mean?"

"Look," he said, "if we'd met normally, I would've, I don't know, asked you out for coffee. Dinner. Gotten to know you the way people do. Instead, here I was living in your house, hired to look for something you didn't know you had."

"Only it turned out, unfortunately for you, that I *did* know. Bad luck, that."

"Indeed. What are the chances that Idrisov would leave that notebook with somebody who could, first, read it, and second, figure out why it was so important? *I* didn't know why Hank wanted it so badly, or why some linguistics professor was chasing after you for it."

"Yes, well, I guess you know now."

"Yes. And I've talked to Hank." He took a deep breath. "Sienna, that notebook has to be destroyed…" His eyes slid sideways. "*Must* you play with that damned pistol while we're talking?"

"Oh. Sorry. What do you mean, it has to be destroyed?"

"For one thing, it's the only thing that'll get Osborne off your back. The man's crazy, and he's dangerous, and he won't give up otherwise. I don't want you to get hurt. And I *really* don't want somebody like that to have the kind of power he could get from studying those notes."

"What are you planning to do?" I wanted to trust him. I dared not trust him. "Some kind of substitution game? I hand over the notebook, you make a show of destroying it in front of Osborne, but somehow you slip it to your boss instead?"

"No. Hank agrees with me. It's too explosive; he'd rather lose it than know the information is out there for someone like Osborne to take advantage of."

I thought that over for a full count of five in Modern Greek: *ena, dhio, tria, tessera, pente.*

"Fine. Go away. Come Monday, I'll get in touch with Osborne and set the notebook on fire in front of him."

"I can't let you take that risk," Michael said. "You have to let me help you."

I felt the cool, hard shape of the pistol under my hand. "Wrong."

His eyes went to my right hand. "Damn it, Sienna, why do I always wind up in your sights instead of that bastard Osborne?"

"Good question! Maybe you should ask yourself that!"

"No, maybe you should—" He stopped, blew out his breath in a hard *huff,* and started over. "Let me help you. Please let me help you, Sienna. That man has no scruples. How are you going to get close enough to convince him you're destroying the notebook, without giving him another chance to attack you?"

I hadn't actually figured that out yet, but that didn't mean I could trust Michael, did it? "That's my problem. You are not involved."

"I can't *not* be involved, now that I know you, now that I know what's going on. Sienna, *please*—"

"Just. Go. Away."

He stood up and hefted the duffel. "All right." He reached in his pocket, dug out the key and dropped it on the floor beside me.

The house seemed very empty after he slammed the front door. I sat on the floor for a long time, listening to the rain drumming on the roof and splashing into puddles outside.

17. We have to stop him

Sunday morning dawned clean and clear and sweet-smelling, all the dust and heat of summer washed away by that cloudburst. It would be back, of course – our first cool days don't come until October and then only if we're lucky – but for the moment I was willing to pretend that summer was over.

If only the summer's problems had been so cleanly washed away.

I still hadn't figured out how I was going to destroy that notebook in front of Osborne. Between worrying about that and wondering if there would be anything left of my minuscule front yard after the storm, I hadn't slept much. I would have been willing to sleep in this morning, but no, here I was twitching and nervous and worrying, and it wasn't even seven a. m.

I made coffee very quietly so as not to wake up Laura, and took myself out onto the front porch, planning to sit in the glider and stare into the coffee mug and gently accustom my system to the concept of being awake this early.

The air smelled sweet and fresh after the rain, and the storm hadn't done as much damage as I feared. The tiny squares of dead grass on either side of the porch steps were still there.

So was a little red sports car parked against the curb.

I narrowed my eyes. Michael had stomped off hours ago. Why—

I went down the steps and rapped on the driver's-side window.

The dark-haired man who was curled up with his head on a duffel bag straightened violently, banged his elbow on the steering wheel, sat up and lowered the window.

"Is that for me?" He reached for the mug that I happened to be holding.

"What are you doing here? I thought you left."

"I'm not in the house, okay? You don't own the street. Gimme."

His bloodshot eyes made a decent case that his need for coffee was even greater than mine. I let him have the mug. He tilted his head back, inhaled a stream of coffee, yelped and plopped the mug on the dashboard.

"Wha' the hell! You s'ill ma' a' me? Tha' burn' my 'ongue!"

"Serves you right for gulping. Can't you wait until it gets cool enough to drink?"

"Tha's wha' milk is for!"

"Wimp."

He inhaled and exhaled several times, passing cool air over his tongue. "That's my thanks for sitting here all night watching for Osborne? An attack with scalding coffee?"

I thought about pointing out that he'd asked for the coffee. And that I had not asked him to sit guard outside the house. Then I thought that this was a stupid argument to be having in the street. My nosy next-door neighbor, Jenn, was probably flapping her ears already. "Oh, stop complaining and come inside. I'll give you some more coffee. With milk. Ice cubes too, if you like."

I wound up making pancakes as well. I'd been missing too many meals lately, and I didn't feel up to going out in public. Besides, I figured it would be easier to finish this fight in the privacy of the kitchen.

That may have been a mistake. The smells and sounds of cooking brought a heavy-eyed Laura out of her side of the house, wrapped in a dark red brocade robe that probably cost more than my entire wardrobe.

"Blueberries," she mumbled through her first cup of coffee, waving at the refrigerator. Those were an excellent addition to the rather boring pancakes from a mix. Given the cost of blueberries here – they probably had to be flown in from some place like Maine – I felt rather as if I were pouring a basket of gold nuggets into the pancake mix. Oh well, they were Laura's gold nuggets.

"Syrup?" Michael asked.

I rummaged through the pantry and came up with two bottles: one plastic bottle of IHOP syrup and one glass bottle that claimed to contain authentic Vermont maple syrup. Laura's, of course.

By the time we were all working our way through a breakfast made luxurious by Laura's contributions, the fight had fizzled into a strategy planning session. How could I safely and nonviolently convince Osborne that the notebook no longer existed?

"Have Michael hold your gun on him while you rip out the pages and burn them in the fireplace?"

"Laura, what part of nonviolent didn't you hear?"

"Well, he doesn't necessarily have to *shoot* him."

"And I don't want Osborne inside this house."

"When was the last time you used the fireplace?" Michael asked while getting himself another half-cup of coffee. He added enough milk that I wasn't sure the result even counted as coffee any more.

Laura started counting on her fingers. "It was cold enough for a fire that time it snowed..."

"The year after we graduated," I contributed, and then, remembering more, "but we didn't actually build a fire, because we didn't have any wood."

"I vote against the fireplace, then," Michael said, "it's probably clogged up with birds' nests."

Remembering Cath Palug's habit of staring into the empty fireplace and swishing his tail at the recurring spring sounds of twittering and fluttering, I had to agree with him.

Maybe one of us knew somebody with an outdoor grill?

"And burning books is harder than you'd think," Michael added. "Unless you tear out the pages and crumple them up..."

Problems, problems. Yes, I could probably use Old Shaimaki to make the notebook burn up. But I wasn't really eager to court brain damage yet again. Defending myself against Osborne yesterday had been...

"First we have to find Dr. Osborne," I said. "He might have been hospitalized; I'm not sure just how badly he was burned."

But he'd used the Language to whisk himself home. Maybe he was still there?

"I'll call," Michael said, pulling out his phone. "What's his number?"

I read it off the backlog of messages on my own phone.

But he didn't answer Michael's call.

"He probably thinks you're a solicitor," I said. "He'll pick up for me."

But I was wrong about that.

I began worrying that I'd killed him with that fire attack.

"Good," Laura said, "that solves the problem."

Michael put his arm around my shoulders. I actually didn't mind. "No. Sienna doesn't need to have killed anybody. Anyway, she can't have. He was alive enough when he disappeared yesterday, Sienna. You didn't burn him nearly enough to have killed him. I doubt he was even hospitalized. It was only a few seconds; at worst, today he'll be feeling like somebody with a really bad sunburn."

I liked that theory, but I still felt shaky. "Old people's skin is thinner…" Now I really wanted to know that Osborne was still alive. I couldn't wait until Monday. A little searching got me Sammy's big sister's number, so I called Mira Martinez next.

"You're looking for Dr. Osborne? That's funny!"

"Why, is he looking for me?" But he knew where I was.

"No, I just mean you're only a couple of hours too late. Cassie and Frank and I all got a text from him this morning. He's leaving the country and may not be back for the beginning of the semester, so we get to cover *all* his lectures instead of just *most* of them."

"Can he do that?"

"There isn't much the holder of an endowed chair can't do," Mira said grimly. "And all three of us are trying to get him to approve our dissertations, so we don't dare *not* cover for him. The –"

She broke into a string of Spanish which significantly added to my vocabulary, but the translation would do nothing for the tone of this document.

"Where is he going?"

"He said research. So, probably one of the 'stans. I'm sure we'll hear *all* about it when he deigns to come back."

After I got off the phone, Michael and Laura and I stared at each other.

"Well, at least he won't be stalking me for the notebook," I said, lifting my hands and letting them fall on the tabletop.

"Worse," Michael said. "Your success in using the Language yesterday must have made up his mind. He's not going to settle for third-hand field notes; he's going to the source."

"Taklanistan."

"The village. Shaimak."

"We have to warn them," Michael said.

"How?" Laura asked. "I doubt they have phones."

"We have to *stop* him," I said.

"How?" Laura asked again.

"We have to go there." That was Michael, getting in half a breath ahead of me. Before Laura could ask again, I answered her.

"I can get a mortgage on the house." Whether I could ever pay it off, that was another question. One I refused to think about, for fear of chickening out.

18. Words of power

Zardusht Timurov, headman of Shaimak village, listened with a frown as the village cleric translated the visitor's demands. The most learned man in the village, Muloqot Parsa was able to turn the foreigner's stilted Farsi into comprehensible Taklan far faster than Zardusht could have puzzled out the meaning for himself.

But he hoped the Muloqot had misunderstood…

"Grandfather, he has translated rightly," piped up little Rukshana, who had no business even being present at a meeting of the elders, much less speaking up so pertly. But in this desperate situation Zardusht would listen to anybody.

"Remember the foreigner who came here last year, the one who died?" she went on.

"He died of the mountain sickness," Zardusht said quickly. "It had nothing to do with us or with… anything else."

He avoided meeting Rukshana's eyes. In fact, all the men of the council seemed to be looking away from them. They all knew that what killed the German professor had not been the mountain sickness. It had been overuse of the Old Language.

"Perhaps this one, too, will destroy himself by using the Old Language," Rukshana said.

"If we meet his demands, and teach it to him?" It was a cheering thought.

The American had begun, insultingly, by demanding food and shelter. As though the Shaimaki were barbarians who did not understand the laws of hospitality to a guest! Even a blood-enemy, arriving at evening, would have been given bread and salt and a place to sleep. Of course, he might have been followed from the village and killed on the next day.

This man was worse than a blood-enemy. But if he spoke truth, killing him would be a disaster to the village.

They had destroyed the talking-machine belonging to the German professor, and had thought that with his death the danger was over. Now there came this American who claimed that the German had made written notes as well as recording the Old Language with his talking-machine. That he, this man called Os-Born, had transcribed the notes and that if he did not return safely to America, they would be published for any fool to read and use. That the same consequence would follow if they refused to teach him more of the Old Language.

"He might have been lying?" one of the council members suggested.

Zardusht shook his head. "He knows something of the Old Language. Remember when he said '*Bu prdmt vla!!mqd bze kzmtq?*'"

"Except he didn't say exactly that, Grandfather," put in Rukshana. "He said—"

"*Stop!*" Zardusht and the Muloqot shouted simultaneously. Rukshana put her fingers over her mouth and blinked away tears.

"I only meant—"

"I apologize for this impertinent child," Zardusht talked over her. "Clearly her parents have failed twice over, once when they allowed her to play with Adjdaak and again when they omitted to beat her soundly for bringing what she learned from him back to the village. *No one* under the age of discretion should ever be allowed to keep company with Adjdaak."

"She amuses him," Rukshana's father mumbled. "Especially now that he cannot travel. In his boredom he would have cost us many more sheep if it were not for Rukshana's distracting him."

"We can afford to lose sheep," Zardusht said loftily. "We cannot afford the destruction that would be spread by children using the Old Language. My son, do you *want* your daughter to end like Simple Ali?"

"Rukshana has better sense than that!"

"I have seen little evidence of it! Perhaps I did not beat *you* enough, eh?"

"Grandfather, uncle, are we not forgetting the immediate problem?" said Muloqot Parsa. Despite the stature granted by his title, sometimes he still felt like the weedy, lame boy who had been sent away to school in Tireza because he was so useless in the fields. Especially when he had to join a village council composed largely of the men who had made that decision.

Zardusht glowered at his son and promised that they would revisit the matter of Rukshana later. Then, with a sigh, he returned to considering the problem of Os-Born.

The evasion they had used with the German, trying to teach him only the roundabout verb forms that would not change the material world, would do them no good with this man. He had already demonstrated that he knew better than to say the safe sentence *Bu prdmt vla!!mqd bze kzmtq,* or 'This thing might disappear'. Instead he had said, correctly, *Bu prdmt vlaad kzmtq,* or 'This thing becomes nowhere'. And the rock he'd picked up had disappeared.

"If he already knows so much," Muloqot Parsa suggested, "perhaps it is best to teach him more – much more – and to hope that he uses it too freely, so that he kills himself like the German."

"I have a better idea," Zardusht's son said. "Let us teach him words of great power and tell him that they are only little words of small power. Then he will not be afraid to use them, and he will hurt himself much more than he is prepared for."

"Suns and Dragons have mercy upon me," Zardusht said mildly, "I am accursed in my old age to preside over a council of babbling idiots. Do you not remember what will happen if the American fails to return to his own country?" His voice grew sharp as a whiplash. "That which this foreigner already knows will be *published,*" (he used the English word) "and every fool will use the Old Language as he likes. The world will be darkened and twisted until all vanishes. But first what horrors will we see? Our women becoming boys, our children turned into birds? The structure of the world warped beyond recognition? I myself," he concluded with a return to his pose of mild reasonableness, "would prefer not to be witness to those last days. But you may differ."

"Very fine to make speeches," grumbled a middle-aged man, "when it was our headman's own family who brought all this trouble on us!"

That aroused a babble of argument and tracings of genealogical lines, in which the grumbler proved conclusively that Koshan Idrisov, the guide who'd brought the old German to Shaimak, was a second cousin to Rukshana's mother's sister's husband in Tireza on the far side of the pass, and Zardusht argued that by such relaxed standards of kinship everybody in the High Pamirs was related to everybody else, and Rukshana's father added that *his* family was innocent of any wrongdoing and they barely knew Koshan anyway.

"But I used to play with him..." Rukshana murmured, "when his family came to the high valleys every summer..."

The quarreling men ignored her until she raised her voice. "Where *is* Koshan now?"

"Ashamed to show his face in the mountains, I suppose," said her father, dusting his hands together as if to shake off that unworthy not-really-a-kinsman.

"No, he went to Merika and sold our language to this Os-Born!"

"Did he know any more of it than the German learned?"

All the men stared at Rukshana.

"We- never- I never told Koshan about the Dragon of Shaimak!"

"But did you teach him any of the dragon's language?"

Rukshana vowed she had never done that, and brought chronology to her aid. "Our aunt used to tell him to watch me, when he was fifteen and I was six, yes! But I never visited Adjdaak until I was more than ten years old, and by then Koshan had gone away to Merzadeh and I never saw him again until last year."

That initiated another argument about the folly of Rukshana's parents, letting the child play around the dragon when she was far too young to be apprenticed to him to learn the old language properly.

Finally Zardusht sighed. "Then all that Os-Born knows is what was in the German's notes. And *he* was not here long enough to learn very much."

"He learned enough to kill himself with it," the Muloqot reminded them.

"Perhaps," one of the men said, "Adjdaak will be angry that a foreigner tries to learn his language. Perhaps Adjdaak will deal with him as he did with those fools who tried to blow up the lake and flood the whole world."

"And then what he does already know will be *published*."

"What does that mean exactly?"

"I think it means that they will make a book of it for anybody to read."

"Would that be so bad? How many people can read?"

"Os-Born claims that all the people in Merika can read."

"Well, that is obviously a lie."

"Even if it is only a few – there are many, many people there. They say there are more people in Merika than in Merzadeh! A hundred times more!"

"That too is probably a lie. Think what great herds of sheep and yaks they would need."

The meeting ended without any satisfactory strategy for dealing with the American, except that everybody would be very polite, and very stupid, and very ignorant, until they worked out what to do.

19. Vodka and ammunition

Apart from a sprinkling of bombed or burnt-out buildings, the capital of Taklanistan didn't look like a place that had been in the run-up to a second civil war when Thalia was there. The ruined buildings were mostly in the process of being torn down or repaired, shops were open everywhere, young people strolled in the parks and children in simple uniforms marched quietly off to school. Jennifer McAusland, Thalia's contact at the American Embassy, commented that you did have to say one thing for competent dictators: when they succeeded in stifling a war, they did so quickly and efficiently.

"And the rebels would have been even more dictatorial," she said, "so on the whole, I'd call this a happy ending." She gave a tiny sigh. "Of course, life was more *interesting* when there was shooting in the streets… The only fun I have now is going up to Gundiz Fort." Last year, while Thalia and her husband had been preoccupied with little things like being taken hostage (Thalia) and trying to effect a hostage rescue without getting the Lake Shaimak dam destroyed (Lensky) Jennifer had found time for a romantic hookup with the Russian officer in command of the border fort at Gundiz. The good part about this, from our perspective, was that she had exceedingly good relations with everybody in Merzadeh who had business in this Gundiz place. She said it would be easy for her to get a helicopter ride there, and we could tag along with her.

"Why a Russian?" I muttered to Michael while she was telephoning around her contacts.

"He's probably lonely."

"No, I mean, what's a Russian army officer doing in Taklanistan?"

"They help the Taklans guard the Afghan border," Jennifer explained between telephone calls. "But I don't know how much longer that's going to last. They could withdraw their people any time if they decide it's cheaper just to guard their own border and let Taklanistan get flooded with drugs and religious fanatics."

A potentially doomed romance, then.

The prospect didn't seem to bother Jennifer much. From the way she was joking with the people she called to bum a ride, the Russian romance also didn't cramp her style that much; to get us three seats on a helicopter leaving tomorrow, she promised somebody a dinner date when he got back to Merzadeh. To get us passes for travel into the Lake Shaimak Restricted Area, she agreed to get a Taklan official a season pass for two to the State Opera and to keep him company at the opening performance of *Aida*.

"Could be worse," she said, putting the phone down. "The second opera on this year's list is a local composition. Interpretive dance, a dramatization of Supreme Leader Ergashi's conquest of the rebels last year, and atonal music. If he'd asked me to go to that, you two would be stuck waiting in line for your travel passes and trying to figure out who to bribe. See you tomorrow. I'll pick you up at seven."

That left us with a free afternoon in the capital of Taklanistan. I looked at the handful of leaflets I'd picked up on the ground floor of the embassy. "We could go see the aluminum plant, I guess. Or the Palace of National Culture." I yawned. "Or go back to sleep."

"*No*," Michael said. "If you want to get over jet lag, you need to stay awake for the rest of the day and go to sleep at a normal time. Besides, we have something more important than tourism to work on."

"We do?"

"We know now that Osborne didn't go through the embassy."

"Do we? Maybe he did. Could be that Jennifer McAusland just wasn't in on that."

"Given her taste for helicopter rides into the mountains, I expect that lady knows all about any travel into the Pamirs that's connected with the embassy.

We need to talk to the people who organize mountain treks." He took the leaflets from me and ruffled through them. "Three outfits left their ads with the embassy – Pamir Expeditions, Silk Road, Roof of the World. Shiny brochures with beautiful color photographs. These are probably the major players, and I bet they can get permits for their customers to explore restricted areas."

I squinted at the fine print under a picture of snow-capped mountains and an improbably blue lake. "Michael, they're aimed at *hikers*. I don't think that's exactly Osborne's style."

"They do jeep tours too. At least, Silk Road and Roof of the World do. Look on the back page. See, they attract tourists with the beautiful scenery and the romance of boldly going on foot into the back country... then they rent jeeps and drivers to the people who suddenly realize they're not actually up for carrying a huge backpack and plodding to the top of the pass."

Well, we had time to check it out, he was right about that. And I felt that Michael had kind of a right to take the lead here, because I hadn't, after all, mortgaged my house to get us to Taklanistan. While Aunt Georgia was still telling me what a terrible idea that was, Michael's boss Hank had turned up in Austin and volunteered to pay our way. Possibly in response to some prodding from Michael, though neither of them admitted that.

Unlike Michael, Hank was a sweetie. I trusted him as soon as we met, and I felt really sorry that he couldn't join us on this expedition. But as he himself admitted, his health wasn't that great; he'd slow us down, and he probably shouldn't take himself and his pacemaker into the High Pamirs at all. I'd promised to take a ton of pictures and videos for him.

We lucked out at our second stop. Not only had Edward Osborne hired a guide and a jeep and gotten his permits issued by Silk Road, but they'd made a similar arrangement six months earlier for a German professor whose guide had been Koshan Idrisov.

That information didn't come via the management, who preferred not to talk about it; Michael picked up a hint about it from a guide who was hanging around the office, hoping for work, and we took him out for a late lunch to pick his brains.

"The boss doesn't like us talking about that trip," Farzad told us over shish kebabs and pilau. "It didn't end well; the old foreigner died of altitude sickness. It absolutely wasn't our fault, he must have had a heart problem and he shouldn't have been bounding around in the mountains – Koshan *tried* to get him to rest, but he was a stubborn man. And he got into it with the villagers: I wasn't there at the time, but apparently they had some kind of superstitious fear of his little recording device and they broke it. He lost his temper and – well – he should never have been there in the first place," Farzad concluded.

"Why did he want to go up to Shaimak, anyway?" Michael asked.

"Koshan said he wanted to study the language."

Michael and I did not look at each other.

"But the villagers didn't want him to?"

"Ignorant mountain people." Farzad shrugged. "They probably thought he was stealing their voices by recording them, or maybe that the voices coming back out of the recorder proved it was full of demons. The German was nuts, anyway. There are plenty of dialects of Taklan in places that aren't so high up in the mountains. He could have studied one of them and gone home safely."

"Is there any possibility that the villagers killed him?" Michael asked.

Farzad shook his head. "No way. I told you, altitude sickness. Koshan was with him all afternoon; he got worse so quickly! He was incoherent by the time Naraiman and I came back. And we were with him, all three of us, when he died."

"Then what?"

"We packed up his things and his body and came straight back to Merzadeh. It was getting hot, and the Germans said he had no relatives to ask for the body, so he was buried in the foreign cemetery out on the Gundiz road."

"What happened to his things?"

"I have no idea. They would have been sent back to Germany, but since there were no kinfolk, the boss probably threw them away. Eventually."

I was having a *really* hard time not looking at Michael.

After we parted from Farzad, we went for a walk. I don't know about Michael, but I really needed to stay vertical and moving if I wasn't going to fall asleep. We wandered down a noisy street full of stores and blaring with music, turned off along the river to get away from the boom boxes, and stumbled upon the city's flower market. Stalls filled with bouquets in brilliant colors surrounded us.

"Roses? This late in the summer?" I stopped and inhaled deeply. The flowers looked small compared to American hybrid roses, but their scent was much stronger.

"What do you think about Farzad's story?" Michael asked. I looked at him over bundles of little purple blooms that looked kind of like bachelor's buttons.

"I think that *if* this German was studying Old Shaimaki, and *if* he took notes as well as making recordings, Koshan could have stolen the notebook without anybody else noticing or caring. In fact," I said, "it's the only explanation I can think of for a field notebook of Old Shaimaki words and phrases… in German script, with German annotations!"

"Yes, that's obvious," Michael said absently. He sniffed a bunch of rust-colored chrysanthemums. "Mmm, smells like autumn… What I found really interesting was what Farzad said about the attitude of the villagers."

"Ignorant? Superstitious?"

"That's his interpretation. I can think of another reason why they'd break the German's recording device, can't you?"

I could, and it cheered me up considerably. "They don't want their language made public." I couldn't keep the smile from my face. "Maybe they'll kill Dr. Osborne."

"Bloodthirsty wench! I'd settle for them convincing him that they don't know any such language, and that he's in the wrong mountain village."

"That would be good too."

We didn't know, then, what he was using to blackmail the villagers into teaching him Old Shaimaki.

Jennifer McAusland turned out to be one of those people who is obnoxiously bright and cheerful first thing in the morning. Michael had tendencies that way too, but at least he needed coffee to get going. And since the hotel only served black coffee, which he considered undrinkable, his cheerfulness was muted. Mine, at seven in the morning, was nonexistent. I didn't even have the energy to ask Jennifer why she'd told us to wear our coats and to buy warm hats and scarves in one of the local markets. I mean, even at this hour it was barely pleasantly cool in Merzadeh.

Halfway through the helicopter ride I found out. The thing climbed, and kept on climbing, and my ears popped in the thin, cold air. So did pieces of the helicopter. I tried to ignore Jennifer's breezy travelogue. She appeared to be on a first-name basis with each mountain that we nearly collided with. Me, I was regretting that morning coffee. I would have been happier with an empty stomach and less vivid awareness of my surroundings, which appeared to be trying to kill us.

"I don't know what it is about Americans back home," Jennifer said sadly after I squeezed my eyes shut and begged her not to tell me about any more mountain peaks. "Y'all seem to have no sense of adventure. Lensky was a party pooper too: he hated this trip and he had the nerve to complain about my driving."

That sounded ominous, given that the plan was for us to borrow a jeep from the fort at Gundiz and drive up into the High Pamirs. I had assumed Michael would insist on driving, but now it looked like he might have to arm-wrestle Jennifer for the keys.

Jennifer had a brief, passionate reunion with her Russian boyfriend at the fort, but when she started making promises for "when we get back," the colonel announced that he was coming with us.

I wondered if he would want to drive, but he handed the keys to Jennifer and told her to warm up the vehicle while he collected supplies. The "supplies" consisted of approximately equal quantities of vodka and ammunition for the two machine guns he brought and the pistol on his hip.

"I hope he doesn't drink and drive," I murmured to Michael while the colonel and his aide loaded the supplies.

"*I* hope he doesn't drink and *shoot*," Michael said. "This guy could be an even worse menace than you."

"Hey. I made a perfect grouping at the range, remember?"

"You probably cheated. Is there a way to say, 'I am a superb marksman,' in Old Shaimaki?"

"If there is, I don't know it," I said truthfully. I felt no need to explain what Old Shaimaki sentence I had actually used.

20. The lake of the dragon

Jennifer drove, with Colonel Grisha sitting beside her. When he wasn't drinking vodka or singing, he gave us a quick tour of agriculture in the Pamirs. When I wasn't praying as Jennifer swung the jeep out to a sharp edge of the road to avoid ruts or boulders, I tried to pay attention.

In the Gundiz valley the harvest was already gathered in, and most villages had even threshed their grain with the help of patient oxen trudging in a circle. Now, outside little mud-brick villages, we saw fountains of pale gold grain rising in the air and falling again. Grisha slewed round in his seat to explain to us that today's stiff breeze made perfect conditions for the first winnowing of the grain. Men with wooden pitchforks stood in a circle around a pile of grain, tossing it in the air for the wind to blow away the chaff. After this first pass, women would spend laborious hours letting streams of grain fall from their hands into baskets, again letting the breeze blow away the lightweight husks.

"You'd think they would have a machine to do that," Michael commented.

"They did once. In the days of the Soviet Union my country gave them agricultural machinery. Then there was the civil war, and things broke down because no one knew how to fix them, and they could not get parts, and the machines rusted in the fields, and now they have to relearn the old ways of their ancestors. Russia is too poor now to give new machines."

"What about American aid?"

Grisha spat out the window of the jeep and made some pungent comments about the corruption of the current regime.

The brilliant blue autumn sky set off the cascades of pale golden grain and the bright rust and gold flowers outside most of the houses. They made a cheerful picture, almost idyllic. But when you thought about blistered hands and aching backs and the incredible boredom of spending all day bending, lifting and tossing, it didn't seem quite so idyllic. I wondered whether the Shaimaki had a sentence or two to help with threshing and winnowing.

Where the folds of the surrounding hills made some shelter against the wind, there were orchards. "Apples," Grisha said, "plums, even apricots. This is a rich valley." We whizzed through a village where women sitting in their front yards peeled and sliced the fruit and laid it out on trays to dry.

Half a bottle of vodka later, the road climbed through a stony wilderness to level out again at a higher altitude. Here the threshing was still going on, and people were picking the last apples from their trees.

Past the boundary of the Lake Shaimak Restricted Area, we had climbed so high that only mulberry trees remained, sprinkled among ripening fields where children ran and threw stones to keep away the birds. The jeep slowed, then came to a stop. I looked around and saw nothing but barren mountainsides, including the cliff that rose precipitously to one side of the jeep and fell equally precipitously on the other.

Grisha interrupted his spirited rendering of "New York, New York," to say, "Are you sure this is a good idea?"

Oh. Just ahead, the right-hand cliff bellied out, forcing vehicles – like the one I was sitting in – to swerve onto a snow-covered patch where the left-hand cliff, I hoped, curved out leftwards to match the other one. There was barely enough room for the jeep to creep across.

"I think it's solid," Jennifer said. "Wait a minute, I'll test it." She grabbed one of Grisha's rifles, hopped out of the car, and walked slowly forwards, jabbing the barrel of the gun downwards at intervals. Grisha moaned. I wasn't sure what made him more unhappy, Jennifer's risking herself or the prospect of snow filling the business end of his rifle.

Where the road resumed, she came back, grinning. "Solid all the way!"

At least she took the curve slowly.

The bad thing about that was that I was sitting on the left, so I had plenty of time to look at where we'd fall when the road failed. If the cliff really curved outwards underneath us, it must curve back right away: I could look straight down into the abyss. I wrenched my gaze back to the inside of the jeep and saw that Grisha was upending a vodka bottle into his open mouth. I considered asking him to pass it back to us.

Once we were back on the regular "road," Jennifer pressed on the accelerator and the jeep roared forwards. Making up for lost time?

Grisha switched to "I'm dreaming of a white Christmas." His knowledge of American popular songs was impressive. Next time the jeep slowed, he interrupted his singing to say, "Almost at Shaimak village now," and to point out the vast blue lake stretching along the north side of the road. "Lake Shaimak – the Lake of the Dragon."

"And how," Jennifer put in.

"What d'you mean?"

Grisha laughed and offered us the vodka bottle. "Did you not tell them?" he asked Jennifer.

"They'd think I was crazy."

Oh, I already thought that. She might have shown respect for the latest hazard, but she hadn't slowed for boulders, ditches, or the occasional would-be hitchhiker trudging along the side of the road. If the colonel didn't object to what her driving style did to the army's jeep, that was his business. But I was a little worried about having my teeth rattled out of my head.

"Ah, you Americans. The 'show-me' people, yes?"

"That's just Missouri," Michael said.

"No, you are all like that. Just wait, then. You will see, then you will believe. In Camelot," Grisha started singing, "the rain may never..."

Not much rain today, at least. But as we rounded a mountain outcropping Jennifer stood on the brakes and the jeep came to a squealing stop, slewing round until it blocked the road. In front of us stood several scowling men and a young girl.

Jennifer said something that I thought translated as, "What kind of hospitality do you call this?" After navigating Merzadeh, I was beginning to get a handle on Taklan-flavored Farsi: a lot of slurred word endings, and a lot of Russian loanwords.

One of the men gently pushed the girl forward. She held out a basket containing a single loaf of bread.

"Rukshana?" Jennifer asked. She got out of the jeep.

"We give bread and salt and a place to rest," Rukshana said in heavily accented English. "But you please not come into village now. There is trouble."

That apparently used up her English, because she and Jennifer went into a quick exchange in Taklan – well, the Taklan version of Farsi. I might be starting to develop an ear for it, but they talked too fast for me. I heard something that sounded like "Osborne" more than once. Then Jennifer got back into the jeep, nodding, and wrenched the wheel to the right, at an angle to the road. As we followed Rukshana up a piece of mountain that was slightly less steep than the rest of the terrain off the road, Jennifer explained what was going on.

"Your Professor Osborne seems to have freaked them out."

"Not ours," I said quickly. "You know that. Did you tell them we've come to stop him?"

"Yes, but I'm not sure they believed me. It seems Professor Osborne told them that he has the German researcher's written notes on some language, and threatened to publish what he does have unless they teach him more of the language. He also said that the notes would be published if he did not return home."

"Old Shaimaki! But he's lying about the notebook. *I* have that."

"Well, you're about to meet a native speaker. You can tell him all about it."

The pitiful excuse for a road came to an end between two stony outcroppings. We grabbed our packs and followed Rukshana, single file, along a footpath that skirted the highest hill and wound around and down towards a sea of blue.

"Lake Shaimak," Rukshana said, pointing downwards.

A few minutes later we could see a cluster of houses climbing the side of the hill behind us.

"Shaimak."

Apparently they wanted us to go around the village. That was okay with me; I would just as soon not face Osborne again until the villagers understood that we were on their side.

For a while the path sloped so steeply downhill that I had to keep all my attention on picking the next step. My knees were quivering when it finally leveled out enough that I could look up again.

Another path joined ours here. It looked as if it led straight back to the village. Before us, a tumble of gray boulders, ranging in size from pumpkin to small house, bordered an expanse of milky blue water that stretched out to a distant horizon. On either side, snow-capped mountains framed the lake.

As we approached the boulders, I realized that one pile actually was a small house – a shelter, anyway. Leaning pillars supported a stone slab over an opening high enough for us to walk inside without ducking, and there were a couple of faded rugs draped over the ground under the slab.

"The... the *shogird* stay here," Rukshana explained. "In summer."

"Shogird?"

"Apprentice," Jennifer McAusland suggested, and Rukshana nodded.

That didn't make a whole lot of sense. 'Apprentice' meant somebody who was learning a craft or a trade, didn't it? What could anybody learn, stuck outside the village with a pile of rocks for company?

"You might want to look again at the rocks," Jennifer said. She and Grisha both appeared to be suppressing a fit of giggles.

Okay, I looked at the rocks. Gray-green boulders, piled up anyhow, some of them gleaming silver as if they were wet. It must have rained earlier.

One of the silver surfaces seemed to undulate and move as I looked at it. I rubbed my eyes. It was... definitely... moving. As it expanded, I saw a fan-like structure of long straight lines, with smooth and very silvery surfaces connecting them...

A wing. It was a wing. And that rounded greenish boulder was a knee, and those quartz shards were claws...

I was backed up against one of the walls of the shelter.

"Adjdaak," Rukshana said. "The Dragon of Shaimak."

"Uh, yes, I see, dragon, okay, that is definitely a dragon." I sounded and felt like a babbling idiot. I shut my mouth with a conscious effort and just took in the shape before me. Fan-shaped scales undulated over a long body, glowing very faintly blue-green along the edges. Claws like long quartz crystals sparkled in the pale sunlight. Long silver fans extended, revealing angular wings that might have been made from some blend of ice and crystals. And eyes that glowed like monstrous topazes looked down on me. How had I ever mistaken this giant, living jewel for a mere pile of rocks?

"Adjdaak might speak now."

A mouth the length of my arm opened, revealing very large, sharp teeth. I tried even harder to melt into the rock at my back. A warm hand took mine. "Breathe," whispered Michael.

Oh. Yeah. Breathing. I remembered how to do that… I thought.

Sounds of rocks clashing together emanated from the dragon's mouth, and I realized how poor my attempts at interpreting the notebook transcriptions had been. Amazing that they'd worked at all.

Breathe.

Now I could pick out subjunctive markers in what the dragon was saying. Most of the vocabulary was beyond me, but the liberal sprinkling of verb endings like *!!mqdi* and the recurring *bze* particle assured me that he was not planning to change the world. And as long as he was talking, he wasn't eating anybody. I relaxed just enough to envy his articulation.

The rock-noises seemed to emanate from very deep in his throat. Did he have an organ there that could pulverize coal? That would be handy for a being that breathed flame, wouldn't it? And over time it could have been adapted to use in generating speech. But then, I hadn't actually seen him making fire. My theory might be all wet.

The flow of words ended abruptly. "He might not like people who try to steal his language," Rukshana announced.

Time for some visual aids. "Tell him we are not stealing it, we are giving it back." I let go of Michael's hand, reached into my tote bag and pulled out the shabby, battered green notebook.

Sounds of tumbled stones came from the dragon.

"What might that be?" Rukshana translated. "It could not be his language."

"It is how humans store his language." I flipped the notebook open and read, "*O!dm vla!!mqd bze bakhsh#*," running my finger along the written words.

The dragon didn't react, so I continued reading. "*M?n. Tsh. Dzlaamk. Djnd vla!!mqd bze dzlaamk.*"

He opened his mouth, so I stopped reading to listen. Whatever he said meant nothing to me, but it made Rukshana giggle.

"He say your accent might be *terrible.*"

"Well, there are some differences between human and dragon anatomy."

Rukshana addressed the dragon and he replied briefly.

"He say that even a stupid little girl like me could speak better."

"Yes, well, there's actually nothing I would like better than to study his language from the source, but unlike Osborne, I respect his privacy."

"*Prdmt bze s'd os born?*"

Ha, I thought so. He could understand me just fine without an interpreter. And even I could figure out what that question meant. I looked at Rukshana. "You have not told him about Osborne?"

"I will tell now," she said. Turning back to the dragon, she launched into a long, complicated-sounding speech. And I had to admit, her accent was loads better than mine.

"He want to know why we have not simply brought this Os-Born to him. He would like a small meal."

While I tried once again to melt into the rock behind me, Rukshana spoke to the dragon again, this time for quite a long while. I could guess what she was telling him when she said "*Dja!mk 'publish' o!dm dve g'#ati.*" Explaining Osborne's threat.

Partway through her speech the dragon made a low rumbling noise. His eyes glowed bright topaz, an orange radiance lit up his mouth and made his teeth look like jagged black silhouettes, and small jets of flame flickered from his nostrils. OK. Fire breather, check. That could be useful. It would be easier to figure out how to use it if I weren't terrified. She kept talking long enough for me to calm myself down by focusing on picking out words and syntactic markers from what she said, and then it was obvious what we needed to do.

When she stopped, I said, "Osborne lied. This notebook I have in my hand is what he claims to have. If Adjdaak could come with us into the village, we could find Osborne and show everybody the notebook and then he could burn it up."

Rukshana said, "He cannot move now."

"How come? Is he under some kind of enchantment?"

She giggled. "No, he is…" She groped for a word, gave it up and started over. "He cannot leave the eggs."

"Eggs!" Was he actually a she?

Rukshana shook her head and explained that Adjdaak's mate - who lived in an even more isolated part of the Pamirs - had come here to lay the eggs, because among dragons it was the job of the male to keep them safe and warm until they hatched. It was a good thing that Adjdaak lived near a village that supplied him with sheep, because sometimes the male starved to death during the months when he could not hunt.

"*Xr!gi qo'r mt vla!!mqd bze ksa#lk b'lng.*"

"*Y#q!* That sheep was *not* sickly, Adjdaak!"

"*Dva z'bik, dva eng q'yn…*"

"It was not either old and tough!"

"*Dva zta!!mqd bze o!dm.*"

"I don't care what you prefer, you promised not to eat people."

Michael moved in front of me.

"He not eat *friend,*" Rukshana said to us.

"For someone who doesn't eat people, he made quite a mess of those terrorists last year," Jennifer McAusland said under her breath.

Oh, great. A seriously good motive for keeping on the dragon's good side, that.

21. A failure of hospitality

There were some smooth boulders, curved just enough to be semi-comfortable to sit on, by the lakeside. We settled down there, where Adjdaak could join in the conversation, to plan our next move.

"Why don't we just go back to the village and put the notebook on an open fire?"

"Is not so easy to burn the books," Colonel Grisha said. "Takes a long time and inside pages don't burn anyway."

"We could tear out the pages and crumple them up."

"What if the wind blows them around?" Jennifer asked. "Do we want to be running all over the village trying to collect the pages?"

"Okay, a regular fire may be more trouble than it's worth. But I think I can destroy the notebook using Old Shaimaki."

It seemed to me to be a reasonable proposition, but this time it was Michael who raised an objection. More than just an objection, really. "You are *not* going to do that, Sienna."

"Why?"

"You don't need to damage your brains any more. It's *hard* to burn books; if the effect on you is proportional to the work you're asking the language to do, you could do yourself permanent harm. You've already pushed your luck far enough. I'll do it. What do I say?"

"You can't afford to damage your brains either," I said nastily, "you haven't got any to spare."

Jennifer whistled. "Low blow, Sienna!"

"Shut up and tell me what to say," Michael snarled.

"How can I tell you if I have to shut up?"

"Dammit, Sienna. Will you just quit arguing already?"

"If you don't want me to say the sentence, how can I teach it to you?"

"One. Word. At a Time." he growled.

"Oh, all right. 'Book is *T!kp*."

"Tikup."

"You put in extra vowels and left out the glottal stop." Actually the *!* symbol was more like a glottal stop followed by a cough. I tried to demonstrate. "*T!kp*."

"Tughkip."

"Um, maybe you'd better just say 'this thing.' That's *bu prdmt*."

"Bu."

"Now say *prdmt.*"

"Purdammit."

At this point Adjdaak said something that made Rukshana giggle. We looked at her for translation.

"Sienna, he say your accent might be bad, but *he* would sound like dying cow and he should forget about using a language he cannot begin to pronounce."

Michael scowled. I felt better. I had not actually been terribly happy about teaching Michael how to do something that was going to hurt him.

"Ok, that gets us back to me doing it. Why don't I—"

"I have other reasons why you shouldn't do it," Michael interrupted, "even if I were willing to let you court brain damage – which I am not. First, if you show people in the village that you can use even one sentence of Old Shaimaki, they might want to kill you. You haven't got the protection of threatening to publish. Second, I don't want you getting anywhere near Osborne. Have you forgotten that he tried to burn you alive last time?"

Men. Evidently he'd forgotten that Osborne was the one who'd gotten scorched. "Fortunately, you're not the boss of me!" I snapped, and then felt like a quarrelsome third-grader. But it was true.

Michael stood up and put both hands on my shoulders. "I am not going to let you go back and sacrifice yourself. You must have serious brain damage already if you think that's a good idea!"

I tried to pull free. He was a *lot* stronger than me.

"It's none of your business what I do! And don't grab me!"

He let go and I jumped up to face him. At least now he couldn't loom over me like that: we were exactly the same height.

"Isn't it, Sienna? *Isn't* it? Didn't you understand what I said when I apologized to you back in Austin?"

"What does *that* have to do with *this*?"

He was standing too close to me. It did funny things to my breathing.

"This is what it has to do with me," he said, and kissed me.

I thought I ought to pull away and slap his face, but my body wasn't cooperating. My arms seemed to be going around him despite what I thought. Then I stopped thinking and kissed him back.

Rukshana giggled again and I stepped back. I could feel my face turning red.

"Is simple," she told us. "Bring Os-Born here, then Adjdaak burn notebook in front of him. Maybe he also burn Os-Born," she suggested cheerfully.

"No! I mean, don't ask him to burn Osborne."

"Sounds good to me," Jennifer McAusland said. "What's the matter, are you squeamish?"

"Very," I told her. Michael was looking a bit green himself, but I resisted the temptation to point that out. "But how do we get him out to the lake?"

"I ask my grandfather. He is very clever man."

***

The Shaimakis were clearly interpreting their tradition of hospitality as narrowly as possible, Osborne thought. True, they had given him a house to stay in rather than making him share one, but he suspected that was because nobody wanted the social contamination of getting too friendly with him. And the house whose family had moved out for him was very small and leaky, plagued with damp spots and infested with surreptitious rustlings that he suspected were rats. He was lucky that he'd loaded the jeep with freeze-dried foods, because the only foods the villagers offered him after the initial bread and salt were a kind of unseasoned porridge and a thin soup of wheat noodles, also unseasoned.

He did occasionally regret having made his Taklan-speaking guide from Silk Road Treks stay behind at the last village before the Lake Shaimak Restricted Area. He didn't want some local finding out about Old Shaimaki. But the drive from there to Shaimak village had been tiring and dangerous, and these stupid peasants kept pretending not to understand the Farsi he'd studied for field work in neighboring Tajikistan. That was where he'd first heard the rumors of an isolated village, high in the Pamirs, where the people knew a language that would work magic. At the time he'd dismissed the stories as a rural myth, not without reason; the tellers embroidered shamelessly, even claiming that the people of Shaimak had learned their magical language from a dragon! But his curiosity about the area had persisted... and then, many years later, the man calling himself Koshan Idrisov had demonstrated the power of the language. He'd made the most of the three scanned pages he'd found on Idrisov's laptop, and although even pronouncing the words kept giving him a headache, the power implicit in those sentences had made him frantic to get hold of the rest of the notebook. But now he had something better than some German's transcriptions! At least he would have, if he could summon up the patience to extract information from these blockheads who had so much trouble understanding him and who kept misinterpreting his questions. They should be able to understand when he spoke slowly; Taklan was nothing but a degenerate dialect of Farsi.

The prospect of power should give him infinite patience. He wasn't about to admit defeat and go home with nothing to show for this expensive jaunt.

When the old, gap-toothed idiot who had spoken most loudly against him sidled up to him behind a house, he wondered if the villagers' resistance to him might be weakening. Up to now no one had approached him, even with the promise of generous payments. And the people he approached all seemed to be involved with dull agricultural and household tasks, too immersed in their work to respond to his questions. This very man, old Zardusht, had tried to excuse them by saying that this was the busy time of year for the village, when they collected and stored up food for the winter. A likely story, when the grain in the fields hadn't yet been reaped!

Now this same Zardusht asked, in his heavily Taklan-accented Farsi, whether Osborne had been serious in his promises of payment to informants.

"The woman of my house desires things from the lowlands," he said, "sugar instead of pounded mulberries, dried apricots as well as our own dried apples, fine bright fabric and boots of leather." He shook his head over the folly of women. "Such luxuries! She is a terrible nag, and it is my shame that I give in to her. But I am an old man, and I desire peace in my house."

Osborne assured him that he would be paid more than enough to buy the 'luxuries' his wife wanted, and backed up that assurance by showing a thick wad of twenty-ergashi notes. Zardusht's eyes brightened.

"Better not to show that to others," he said. "Some people here might kill you for it."

"What a failure of hospitality," Osborne said blandly. He was not seriously worried by the warning. Two days had been enough to assure him that the villagers, although angry and stupid, were thoroughly cowed by his threats of publication should he fail to return on schedule.

"If you want the money," he said into Zardusht's continuing silence, "talk to me."

"I do not want to be seen with you," Zardusht told him. He pointed away from the village. "Do you see that path? It leads to a place beside the lake that cannot be seen from here. I will go now. You follow me after I am no longer in sight. I will meet you and guide you the rest of the way."

Inwardly exulting, Osborne readily agreed.

***

While we waited for Zardusht to bring Dr. Osborne, Adjdaak lowered his head and body to the ground, furled his wings and gave an extremely good imitation of a pile of weathered boulders. Michael and Colonel Grisha took positions on either side of the path where they could grab Osborne as soon as he came around the bend. When Jennifer McAusland complained about being left out of the fun, Grisha suggested that she could gag him with her scarf so that he wouldn't be able to employ whatever scraps of Old Shaimaki he knew.

All I did was hold the battered notebook. My job was to show it to Dr. Osborne and make sure he knew that it was what he'd been seeking. That was one reason the men had to hold Osborne; getting close enough to him to demonstrate what was in the notebook, they said, was too risky otherwise.

Couldn't argue with that.

Once Osborne knew what the notebook was, I was to toss it to Adjdaak, who boasted that he could flambé it in mid-air.

It almost worked out like that.

Dr. Osborne was looking down, watching his step on the uneven ground of the path as it slanted downhill to the lake, when Michael and Grisha jumped him. He started to shout something but Jennifer shoved the end of her scarf into his open mouth and wound the rest of it around his head. He struggled so furiously that his glasses fell off.

I wanted him to have the glasses so that he could see that I really did have the notebook he'd attempted to steal. I ran up to rescue them before somebody stepped on them and he kicked me in the head, hard, with one of his heavy hiking boots. A starburst of pain exploded on the left side of my head and I fell to my hands and knees, dizzy.

When my vision cleared, Michael had his hands around Osborne's neck.

"No, Michael!" I struggled to my feet and grabbed his arm. "Don't kill him!"

"Why not?" Grisha asked.

"Sounds good to me," said Jennifer.

"I don't want you to be a murderer!" I told Michael.

His hands loosened. Osborne was making choked crowing noises. But as soon as Michael let go of his neck, he twisted and drove his elbow into Grisha's belly. The next moment he had freed himself and was running away from us, away from the village, towards the lake.

Behind him came Zardusht, clicking his tongue censoriously. He said something which Rukshana translated for us, just in case I hadn't followed.

"I did not go to the trouble of bringing him here just for you to play with him."

Grisha said several things in Russian which nobody felt the need to translate. I hoped I would be able to remember everything later. They would be a useful addition to my vocabulary; we never learned those kind of words in Intensive Russian, but I could deduce their meaning from the context.

Michael just growled.

And the pile of boulders that Osborne had been making for unfurled vast silvery wings, raised its head, and fixed him with a swirling golden eye. Lazily, as if swatting a pest, he raised one foreleg and trapped Osborne under his extended claws.

He asked Rukshana a question, and she ran to him and knelt beside Osborne. She answered him and then turned to us. "He is not dead. But he is...um..."

"Fainted?" I suggested. "Lost consciousness? Passed out?"

She nodded. "He is fain ted." She made two words out of it.

After that, we had to persuade Adjdaak to raise his claws so that we could pull Osborne out from underneath them, tie him up with my nice warm wool scarf, and splash lake water on his face until his eyes opened.

He looked at Adjdaak and made frantic noises through the gag. I was afraid he would choke, so I unwound Jennifer's scarf and pulled the end out of his mouth.

"Get it away from me," he gasped. "It's not real. I'm hallucinating..."

"Stupid soft thing," Adjdaak roared. "I might be more real than *you* are!"

He spoke English? Well, I'd already guessed he understood it. I guess it was just dragonish intransigence that he'd insisted everything we said had to pass through his language of grinding and crushing sounds.

"Look at this, *Eddie*," I snarled, thrusting the open notebook at him. I might still think of him as Dr. Osborne, but he'd lost the right to be addressed respectfully. "See the German script? Can you read it?"

"*Q!x vlaad —*"

Before he could say whatever disaster he was aiming at me, I slammed the notebook shut and Jennifer shoved her scarf back between his teeth.

"This," I said slowly and clearly, "is the notebook you tried to steal." I looked at Zardusht and tried to add a Taklan flavor to my Farsi. "Grandfather, this is the book. The book Osborne said he would publish. He lied. He does not have anything to publish."

I could tell by the way Zardusht's frown cleared that he understood and believed me.

"Adjdaak!" I called to make sure he was watching. "Here!"

I threw the notebook up in the air, pages ruffling in the wind off the lake. Adjdaak reared up and belched flame into the sky, surrounding the notebook and reducing it to ashes that fell, appropriately, over Edward Osborne.

"Do you think we can ungag him now?" Jennifer asked. "It's getting cold and I'd like my scarf back."

I regretted having donated my own scarf to tie his hands, because I for sure didn't want to untie him.

"You want the gag out of your mouth?" Michael asked Osborne. "Get this straight. You try anything in the dragon's language, and you'll be counting your teeth."

"I think we just shoot him," said Grisha.

"Cut off his tongue," Jennifer suggested.

Didn't these two people have any boundaries? I could understand their romance now; they were the same brand of crazy.

"Eddie," I said, "it won't do you any good to pull out the pitiful scraps of Old Shaimaki you may be able to remember. Even if you could hurt us, the entire village hates you, and now Zardusht can tell them that they don't have to fear your threats. Rukshana, what do your people do to someone who threatens their existence?"

"Give to dragon," she said with a cheerful smile.

Adjdaak rumbled deep in his throat, and little tongues of flame darted from his nostrils. Osborne turned green and fainted again.

"Dammit," Jennifer said, "we'll have to carry him." She pulled her scarf free and looked sadly at the damp bits. "And I'm not sure I want to wear this again."

Michael sat down beside me and put his arm around my shoulders. I realized that I was shaking after all that.

"How's the head? How badly did he hurt you?" he asked while Grisha heaved Osborne's unconscious body across his shoulder.

"See you in the village!" Jennifer called cheerfully, and they started back along the path, preceded by Zardusht and trailed by Rukshana.

"I don't know," I told Michael. "How bad does it look?"

"You're going to have an impressive shiner," he said. "Do you have a headache?"

"Well, it hurts where he kicked me, but that's all."

"Any nausea? Dizziness? Confusion? Do you remember what happened?" He fired off those and more questions rapidly, as if testing my ability to keep up with him. Finally he said, "Well, I don't think you have a concussion, but the dizziness and seeing stars right after he kicked you are not a good sign."

"Oh! Did anybody pick up his glasses?" I suddenly remembered how I'd gotten in a position to be kicked in the first place. He'd been able to see well enough to recognize the notebook anyway, so I didn't care that much about the glasses now.

"Jennifer has them. Look, you're probably going to be all right, but somebody should stay with you tonight and keep checking on you. I'm volunteering. I mean… if that's all right with you?"

"More than all right." I let my aching head rest on his shoulder.

"You know," he said, "when you said you didn't want me to be a murderer… I have killed people before."

"When you were in the army?"

"Yes."

"That's different, though. I mean, it was kind of your job." I thought for a moment. I'd heard other veterans complain about the people who asked if they'd ever killed anybody. "I don't want to hear about it – I mean, if you want to talk about it, that's fine, but you don't need to."

"Well, protecting you is kind of my job now."

I was poised to snap that I didn't need protection. But I couldn't very well start that fight while my head was on his shoulder and he had a warm arm around me, and I didn't want to move just yet.

22. Words of great power

We promised Zardusht that we would leave the next morning.

"And you will take Os-Born with you," he said.

I sighed. "I suppose we must." Though how we were going to manage him I did not know. We could hardly keep him tied and gagged all the way to Gundiz.

"We'll have to," Michael said when I consulted him. I'd waited until the villagers had left us alone in the house where Osborne had stayed, and until he had been moved to a tiny back room where he couldn't eavesdrop on us.

I made a face. "It's going to be messy."

"You don't want him, but you wouldn't let Adjdaak have him either," Jennifer observed. "I call that rather a dog-in-the-manger attitude."

"You don't seriously want to give him up to be *eaten by a dragon!*"

She shrugged. "Why not? In that standoff last year Adjdaak took out three terrorists, and this guy is potentially more dangerous than all three of those nuts."

"I don't think he's learned enough Old Shaimaki to be that dangerous," I said, "and if he uses any strong sentences, his head will hurt and he won't be able to remember what he's doing."

"Are you absolutely sure of that?" Grisha demanded.

Well, no, I wasn't. He was smart and fast; since our encounter at the Rivers house he'd figured out why his Shaimaki sentence hadn't worked and mine had, and he'd generalized that to use indicative when he tried to use the language on me. "The girl becomes —" and the gag had stopped whatever unpleasant condition he'd been about to wish on me.

Even if finishing the sentence might have given him a headache, it might have done something far worse to me.

We thrashed all that out in detail and even I had to admit that if we didn't kill Osborne, we would have to keep him gagged.

But that was only putting off the problem. While we might manage that in the High Pamirs, it was bound to occasion some comment as we got back to civilization. We couldn't keep him under control forever. And Michael and I couldn't quite reconcile ourselves to killing him in cold blood, or handing him over to Adjdaak to kill and eat.

Well, I couldn't, anyway. I wasn't so sure about Michael. By the end of the discussion he seemed to be leaning towards Jennifer's and Grisha's point of view.

Then I remembered something Rukshana had mentioned while chattering to me about that good-looking boy in the Varshas family, the council's deliberations on how to deal with Osborne's demands, the hard work of the upcoming harvest and her grandfather's totally unreasonable ban on using any of the language of the dragon to make the work just a tiny bit easier. I excused myself from the discussion by saying I needed to stretch my legs outdoors before trying to sleep.

Michael, naturally, insisted on coming with me, and I couldn't explain why that was not possible until we were well away from Grisha and Jennifer.

"I've had an idea about Osborne," I told him, "but I need to talk to Rukshana. And her family may not be happy about me taking her for a walk if you're along. They already think she's boy-crazy."

"They're right," Michael said. "If you go for a walk with her, better steer clear of the Varshas house."

I promised to keep her well away from young Rustam Varshas, and Michael consented to skulk along well behind us and keep to the shadows. It seemed like the best deal I was going to get.

Rukshana was delighted to get out of evening chores by going for a walk with The Foreign Lady Who Speaks Taklan, and her mother had no objection. I got the feeling that some things were universal: getting a moody teenage daughter to do her chores was more trouble than doing them yourself.

We picked our way uphill and away from the village until Rukshana found a patch of gently time-worn boulders that were slightly less uncomfortable for sitting on than the rest of the mountainside. "Also, from here you can see everything!" she confided happily. She'd quit trying to improve her English with me in favor of unrestricted chatter in Taklan, most of which I could follow. "There's our house, and Rustam's house, and…"

"And the house your people are letting us stay in," I said quickly, before she could get going again on Rustam's many perfections.

"Old Paikan and Hasti's place," Rukshana said. "They moved in with their son's family. They are happy enough there, but the son's wife can't wait for you to leave so her in-laws can go back to their own house." She giggled. "Zhala says her mother-in-law finds enough to criticize when she's only living next door, having her in the next room is intolerable. But why did Zhala and her man build such a big house, if they didn't want to have relatives stay with them?"

I could think of other reasons for wanting a big house, but I didn't want to get Rukshana started speculating on Zhala's fertility. "No idea," I said, "but I wanted to ask you about something else. This afternoon you mentioned that someone on the council had an idea for tricking Osborne with the language."

She nodded. "It would have been *fun*, too, but my grandfather thought it was too dangerous. It was my father's idea that we should teach him words of great power that would hurt him to use, and tell him they were only words of small power. Then maybe he would make himself mad, or die, from using too much of the language's power. But my grandfather said it might not work, and anyway it would not solve the threat of somebody else publishing the language. That was before we knew that he was lying, you see."

"I have been thinking about that. If someone could teach him to say words that had great power but would do no harm, and tell him they were words that would give him revenge on me – on us…"

"I can think of some!" Rukshana interrupted my slow Farsi. "There are words to bring a warm wind from the south, and others to make the clouds disappear and the sun to shine. Those are good things. They give us more time for the mulberries and wheat to ripen and more time to harvest them before the world freezes. We need those words now, because the harvest is so late. But we have waited and waited, because whoever speaks those words becomes mad. Sometimes they die."

She started to teach me the sentences, safely using only one word at a time, but I stopped her. "I can't tell him. He wouldn't believe me. Maybe your grandfather…?"

Rukshana shook her head. "Zardusht already lied to him once, remember?"

"Your father, then. He should be willing; it was his idea."

"*Nobody* ever listens to my father," Rukshana said. "My mother says that a *shitan* spat between his lips and cursed him that he should never be believed. I have a better idea.…"

"Oh, no," I said when she finished, shocked back into English. "No *way*."

"*Is* way," said Rukshana, pouting, and then reverted to rapid-fire Taklan that I could barely follow, 'explaining' why she was the best person and the only person to deal with Osborne.

"He is dangerous," I said weakly. I couldn't begin to match her fluency and power of exposition in Taklan-Farsi. "If he harms you, your parents will kill us. And they will be right!"

Rukshana's lower lip stuck out so far I could have used it for a bookshelf.

"There must be someone else. Who is there on the council who might do this?"

"Nobody," Rukshana said. "You are taking Os-Born away. He is not their problem now. *I* would help, and I would not even ask you for a dowry."

"Well, that's a good thing, because you're not getting one," I said as sternly as I could. "You're a little girl. It's far too soon for you to think of marriage."

"Rustam Varshas does not think so!"

I made a mental note: never have a teenage daughter. Not that it seemed likely to happen.

I still don't know how she wore me down, but by the time we were both shaking with cold we had the elements of a plan. By that time Michael had given up on skulking at a distance and had joined us; if it weren't for his backing I think I never would have let Rukshana take the risk. We settled that

Rukshana would bring food for all of us and would volunteer to feed Osborne. Michael would go with her to the back room, to watch while she worked on Osborne. She would tell him in Taklanese Farsi – which Michael did not speak, so he could credibly guard them without realizing the plot – that in return for his cash to use as a dowry, she would teach Osborne some words that would give him revenge on us. But she would exact a promise that he wouldn't use them until we were out of the village, because she didn't want to get into trouble with her parents.

"I will pretend to be a silly little girl who thinks him a very fine man," Rukshana said, giggling, "and he will like to believe that, and so he will believe all the rest as well."

She was going to be a dangerous woman when she grew up.

Oh, strike that. Rukshana was dangerous *now*. I underlined my mental note to avoid having a teenage daughter.

***

"You take that off, let him eat," the native girl said to that interfering bastard Michael Ryan, pointing at the scarf gagging him. Ryan looked sour but followed the girl's instructions, adding some of his own: "One syllable out of you and remember what I said before, you'll be counting your teeth." He squatted on the floor, close enough to carry out his threat.

"They are being cruel to you," Rukshana said in slow, carefully clear Taklan.

Osborne nodded. His tongue felt thick and dry. He was in no condition to shape the harsh sounds of Old Shaimaki, even if he hadn't been afraid of Ryan.

Rukshana held a cup for him to drink from – by God, it wasn't just water! This lovely child had spiked it with some of the Russian's vodka! Osborne slurped eagerly, realizing now how much he really needed a drink to help him get over the day's horrors. After that she spooned some bland porridge into his mouth. These peasants really were stupid; with all the power of the language to use, why did they stay in miserable huts and eat this crap? They lived no better than anybody in the other villages of the High Pamirs – and yet they could have been kings.

"People are unkind to me too," said the girl, offering him another sip of 'water.' "My father is poor and my man will not marry me without a dowry."

As if he cared about her problems.

"He is a good-looking man," she went on, "though not as fine as *you*." She patted his shoulder.

Well, no surprise if he'd turned a village maiden's head. He supposed she'd never seen a civilized man before. But what good taste she had, recognizing that he was in a different class from the American and Russian thugs!

"If I told you some words of power," she said, "would you give my dowry?"

He nodded, then glanced at Ryan. The American wasn't even watching them. Of course, he wouldn't know Farsi, let alone the Taklan dialect; he had no idea what the girl was offering him.

"They must be worth it," he said, very low, and keeping his eyes on the American, who seemed to be wrapped in his own thoughts and ignoring them.

"What do you wish? Power, wealth, revenge?"

She could not know any words that would give real wealth, or she'd use them to get her own dowry.

"Revenge," he said. Once he had destroyed these thugs who'd tied him up, he would be able to force the villagers to teach him all he wanted of the language.

"You must promise not to use them until you have left this place," the girl said. "My father and grandfather would be angry and beat me."

So what?

"And they might use their own words of power against *you*."

Very well, it might be best to take his revenge after they were at least out of sight of the village. Then when he returned, these dull peasants wouldn't realize immediately that he had the upper hand of them. He might have to use the revenge words on some of them to encourage the others.

"Tell me."

"My dowry!"

"Take the... flat purse... from my pocket."

Rukshana extricated his wallet and counted the fifty- and twenty- ergashi notes with a pleased smile.

Ryan roused himself. "Hey, what are you doing?"

"The kind gentleman gives me for my dowry," Rukshana said in English.

"Oh, well..." Ryan moved back to the corner of the room and braced himself against the walls, his eyelids drooping.

"These words make your enemy's heart stop," Rukshana said, very low. "First..."

She gave him the phrase "*Iszk zh'm#l kla!d jndb'dn,*" one word at a time. He mouthed the words after her until he felt sure of the whole sentence. It didn't take long. After all, he'd initially specialized in linguistics because he was good at learning languages; before he figured out that linguists in America really didn't like foreign languages, they preferred to believe that everything could be learned by studying English because all languages had identical properties.

"I want more," he told her. "What if I wish one of them to suffer first?"

"Of course," the girl purred, "a great man must see his enemies suffer greatly. This will make a man or woman do your bidding, even if you tell her to kill her lover. Our men use it on faithless wives." And she taught him, "*B#lt zmok uz!qa.*"

By the time she had finished feeding him and left, Ryan was looking very sleepy. He made a gesture towards replacing the gag, but wound it so loosely that Osborne found a little work with his tongue pushed the thing out of his mouth while leaving it over the lower part of his face. With luck they'd never notice that he was now free to speak.

He mouthed the words the girl had given him silently, one word at a time, until the two sentences were indelibly engraved in his memory.

The villagers saw them off in the morning with both jeeps, the Russian one and the one Osborne had hired from Silk Road. That vicious woman from the embassy and her Russian friend took the army jeep. Michael Ryan and that little bitch Sienna took his jeep, relegating him to the back seat. All the better! He would control them first, make Sienna untie him and let Ryan watch while he showed the impudent girl what she deserved for insulting him and trying to destroy his great research project. Then he would stop their hearts. As for the Russian and his American mistress, they could go on back to Gundiz for all he cared, unless they were stupid enough to come back and interfere with him.

The couple in the Russian Army jeep took off first, at a speed that no sane driver would emulate. Ryan drove much more cautiously. Osborne was content to sit in the back for a while, letting the other vehicle get far ahead of them. He counted to one hundred after he could no longer hear sounds from the Russian jeep. That was far enough; he didn't want to have to walk back. Oh, but of course once he had used the control sentence, he could simply get out of the jeep and order Ryan to turn it around. And if the man couldn't do that, and the jeep went over the cliff, well, small loss.

But first he would have some fun. He twitched his chin and wriggled against the seat back until the scarf fell away from his face.

"*B#lt zmok uz!qa,*" he said, low but with perfect enunciation.

A blinding pain shot through his forehead and he fell sideways as the jeep went around a sharp turn. Struggling upright, he was half blinded by the morning sun. Funny, it had been cloudy a moment ago. And why was Ryan still driving? Perhaps because he hadn't yet ordered him to stop?

"Stop!" he said sharply.

There was no reaction from the front seat.

"*B#lt zmok uz!qa!*" he snapped, quite loudly this time. His head hurt even worse, probably because the sun was so bright now and the cold so piercing.

The girl Sienna turned and looked at him. "Did you want something, Eddie?"

"You will not call me Eddie." Now that he had used the words of control, that sort of insolence would be at an end.

"I'd prefer not to call you anything at all. Why don't you shut up?"

It must be necessary to phrase his commands very precisely. She had obeyed him but hadn't given him the cringing respect he meant to extract before humiliating her even farther.

"You are afraid of me."

"You're a menace, that's for sure!"

"And you show me total respect. You acknowledge that you are subservient to me in all things. You obey my lightest word."

"You enjoy a rich fantasy life, don't you, *Eddie?*"

There must have been something wrong with the first phrase. Very well, enough fooling around; his head was splitting, his vision was blurry and he could barely remember the other sentence. Better go ahead and use it before it was too late.

"*Iszk zh'm#l kla!d jndb'dn!*"

The pain this time was incapacitating. He groaned and fell sideways against the seat. Through watering eyes he felt a surprising warmth in the air. Did he have a fever? Why hadn't the couple in front fallen dead already?

"*Iszk zh'm#l kla!d jndb'dn!*"

The world went dark.

***

"It's getting almost warm," Michael said in surprise.

Osborne stirred in the back seat. "*Q!x…*"

I startled, but Osborne's sentence trailed off.

"*Q!x…* what comes next? Who *are* you?" he asked plaintively.

Then again, as though it were burned into his brain too deep to destroy,

"*Iszk zh'm#l kla!d jndb'dn….*" He screamed, then fell sideways onto the seat.

For the next few minutes he alternated between unconsciousness, crying that his head hurt, and babbling that got farther and farther from any possible meaning.

"I hope it's permanent," Michael said viciously.

"I think it probably is. Rukshana told me that those two sentences are so powerful that they're only used in dire necessity, and then the oldest man in the village usually volunteers and makes his son promise to kill him afterwards. It would have been her grandfather – Zardusht – if she hadn't tricked Osborne into using them." I thought for a minute. "And he used them *twice*. One of them three times! I'm surprised he isn't dead already."

"It would be a mercy if he were," said Michael.

"Can you kill a madman in cold blood? I can't."

"What do they mean, anyway?"

"Well… *he* thought the first one would make our wills subordinate to his, that he would be able to make us do whatever he demanded while knowing and hating it inside ourselves." Despite the warming air, I shivered. "He really was an evil man. And the second sentence was supposed to stop our hearts."

"Jesus Christ," Michael said, but reverently, not like he was swearing. "And why were the times so desperate that Zardusht was about to sacrifice himself?"

"You know how cold and cloudy it's been?"

"Up to now?" It certainly wasn't like that any more. In fact, we were almost uncomfortably warm. Michael slowed the jeep to a stop so he could remove his scarf and open up his jacket. I unzipped my jacket too.

"And the harvest was already late. They were afraid it would snow – heavily – before the grain ripened. No harvest, and people die. The old, sick, and the babies for sure. With winter coming on this early, Zardusht would have had to speak those sentences, and they would probably have killed him."

"What do they really do?"

"One of them makes the clouds disappear and the other one makes a warm wind come from the south. I don't know which is which and I don't want to." I shivered again. "At least we don't live where it can be a matter of survival to use them."

A few miles farther on, Osborne's wailing was beginning to get on both our nerves. We agreed that it was safe to untie him and give him a handful of snow to hold against his head with his gloved hand.

"But he comes up in the front seat where I can grab him if he tries anything, and you go in the back where he can't reach you," Michael insisted.

We stopped and made the changeover. I didn't really think Osborne was up to making any more trouble; his babbling sounded like baby sounds now. But I got him some snow as long as I was up. It was so soft now that I had to pack it like a snowball to give him a handful that would last any time at all.

With all these stops, I expected we would be far behind Jennifer and Grisha, but as we rounded a hairpin turn leading to a long straightaway, we saw their vehicle in front of us, although it was a couple of football fields away. Hmm. They must have stopped somewhere too, and it hadn't been to tend to an invalid.

The nasty bit where the cliff bellied out and the road narrowed was at the end of the straight stretch. I watched in horror as the outer wheels of their jeep broke through the snow cover, but Jennifer wrenched the wheel to the left, heading almost into the rocks on the inside of the curve. She speeded up and they made it across the narrow space at the cost of the driver's-side mirror and the jeep's paint job.

Michael pumped the brakes of our jeep very gently and we came to a stop maybe fifty yards from the narrow section, which was now a lot narrower. "The warm wind from the south," he said grimly. "Some of that "solid" support must have been snowpack or ice."

"What do we do now?" I asked. "Reverse all the way to the village and beg them to take us in?"

"Jennifer made it across," he said, "and we have the advantage of knowing what we're up against. And this jeep is a foot narrower than the Russian model, with a correspondingly narrow wheelbase. Also, you're going to walk across before I try it."

"Why don't we all walk?"

"Because those two might be too far ahead by now to notice that we're stranded, and I don't plan to die of hypothermia while we try to walk out of these mountains. I don't plan to die at all."

He got out of the jeep and started throwing things out: the spare tire, the tool kit, our backpacks. "Make it as light as possible before I attempt to cross," he explained.

"Then Osborne had better walk too." I felt just slightly better about getting out of the jeep if it was a matter of lightening the load, not just saving me while he took all the danger.

"Not safe," Michael objected, but he couldn't fault my reasoning. But he insisted on tying Osborne's hands in front of him before letting him go.

"And Fast Eddie here walks ahead of you," he decreed.

Persuading the babbling Osborne to walk ahead, hugging the cliff wall, was no more difficult than persuading a toddler to do the same thing. In other words, it took a long time and some shouting from Michael to get him to set off.

I picked my steps carefully, afraid of hitting a slick patch and sliding off the edge. Osborne, with a toddler's unconcern for danger, strode out confidently ahead of me and walked much too close to the remaining edge.

Halfway around the perilous curve, he turned and frowned at me. "Slow!" he complained.

"Be careful!" I hoped he understood me.

He shook his head and smiled gaily. "Fly," he said, and stepped off the edge, ignoring our warning shouts. I could just hear a sickening thud far, far below.

My knees were trembling. With one hand on the cliff for balance, I made my shaky way to the far side of the curve. Then I sat down on the stony ground.

I could hear the grinding of the jeep against the cliff, and I prayed. Surely fate would not require that we die for letting Osborne fall? "God, please understand that we could not save him… and let Michael pass safely."

No sight in the world had even been more welcome to me than the front of the jeep coming around that bend. I forgot to breathe until the whole of it was on solid ground.

Michael stopped and looked over the edge. "I saw everything," he said. "You had no chance of saving him."

I realized that I was selfishly glad that Osborne had been too far ahead for me to grab him. We would both surely have fallen.

And instead of feeling suitably grieved, I was insanely, joyously exhilarated by our reprieve. And Michael, after that look at the abyss, felt the same way. I tottered to him and his arms went around me and held me up, pressed against his strong, warm body.

"You know," he said after a long, long kiss, "the other two are way far ahead of us now. And the back seat's free… and it's almost warm now."

The dizzy exhilaration still had hold of us both, and… well, awkwardness and cold weren't enough to dissuade me, and neither was common sense. It was probably just as well that Jennifer and Grisha decided to come back up to check on us, though I was slightly disappointed at the time.

"We thought you'd fallen!" Grisha bellowed while they were still a hundred yards away.

Michael put the jeep in gear and drove forward slowly to meet them. He told them what had happened to Osborne.

"Couldn't happen to a nicer guy," was Jennifer's verdict.

Michael squinted at the narrow, slippery road. "What are you guys going to do now? Reverse all the way to the next village?"

"No need," Jennifer said cheerfully, "I only have to back up as far as that wide spot in the road."

It didn't look all that wide to me, but she managed the turnaround. And Grisha said later that it was a base canard to imply that he'd turned green during the process.

"You know," Michael said thoughtfully a long time later, when we were well out of the Shaimak Restricted Area, "now that Osborne is no longer a threat, are you sorry you destroyed that notebook?"

"No!" I said. "Hank was right; it's too dangerous to risk its falling into the wrong hands." Besides, I still had that flash drive with the pictures I'd taken of every page. But he didn't need to know that.

Also by Margaret Ball

Applied Topology series:

A Pocketful of Stars

A quiet math major has to fight in the magical realm for her life and those of her friends after the CIA decides to make use of her paranormal abilities.

An Opening in the Air

When a rival mage attacks, Thalia needs wits as well as magic to save the Center for Applied Topology. And the defense may cost her the man she loves.

An Annoyance of Grackles

It's bad enough when a rival mage tries to destroy you. When he turns out to be a god, that's worse. And when the god teams up with the most notorious contract bomber in America? If Thalia can't outwit the duo, she may wind up scattered across the campus in tiny pieces.

A Tapestry of Fire

Saving her best friend from life as a fish is difficult. Rescuing the man she loves from a past era of fire and fury ought to be impossible, so it may take Thalia a little longer.

A Creature of Smokeless Flame

When CIA officers' children are kidnapped for revenge, Thalia and her colleagues follow the trail across the continents to an African terrorists' camp whose leader has the help of his own personal genie.

A Revolution of Rubies

When Thalia started working directly for the CIA, she didn't expect to follow a trail of stolen rubies to a Central Asian country in the throes of revolution – much less to be taken hostage by the revolutionaries.

Regency Magic series:

Salt Magic
Sabira can deal with her underwater family and with mysterious murders and encroaching sea monsters on land. The hard part is explaining to the man whom she comes to love that she is not exactly human.

Harmony series:

Insurgents
Awakening
Survivors

Earlier books:

Disappearing Act
Duchess of Aquitaine
Mathemagics
Lost in Translation
No Earthly Sunne
Changeweaver
Flameweaver
The Shadow Gate

www.ingramcontent.com/pod-product-compliance
Lightning Source LLC
Chambersburg PA
CBHW032141170626
46808CB00006B/2325